Willam H. H. Murray

The Doom of Mamelons

Willam H. H. Murray

The Doom of Mamelons

ISBN/EAN: 9783337392291

Printed in Europe, USA, Canada, Australia, Japan

Cover: Foto ©Andreas Hilbeck / pixelio.de

More available books at **www.hansebooks.com**

THE

DOOM

OF

MAMELONS.

A LEGEND OF THE SAGUENAY.

W? H? H. MURRAY.

PHILADELPHIA :

HUBBARD BROTHERS, Publishers.

1888.

AUTHOR'S PREFACE.

I have for some years felt that the connection of the old races with the North American Continent, the signs and proofs of whose presence are to be found almost everywhere, and nowhere so frequently as on the St. Lawrence, afforded material for entertaining authorship. Prompted by this feeling, I have, during these several years past, been working at certain pieces of composition, of which this bit of romance is a fair sample.

If it shall so far please the reading public that its publisher shall not lose money by his venture—for letters in our time have no patronage save from the hope of selfish gain—I shall, later on, print others like to it. But if it fail, as it quite likely will, to bring him commercial profit, then they will be forgotten as this one will, until I better them, or they come to a better time.

W. H. H. MURRAY.

BURLINGTON, VT., January 7, 1888.

MAMELONS.[1]

A LEGEND OF THE SAGUENAY.

CHAPTER I.

THE TRAIL.

I T was a long and lonely trail, the southern
end of which John Norton struck in answer to the summons which a tired runner brought him from the north. The man
had made brave running, for when he reached
the trapper's cabin and had placed the birchbark packet in his hands, he staggered to a
pile of skins and dropped heavily on them,
like a hound which, from a three days' chase,

[1] Mamelons. The Indians' name for the mouth of the
Saguenay, and signifies the Place of the Great Mounds.
See note 12.

trails weakly to the hunter's door, spent nigh
to death. So came the runner, running from
the north, and so, spent with his mighty race,
dropped as one dead upon the pile of skins.

He bore the death call of a friend, whose
friendship had been tested on many an am-
bushed trail and the sharp edge of dubious
battle. The call was writ on bark of birch,
thin as the thinnest silk the ancients wove
from gossamer in the old days when weaving
was an art and mystery, and not a sordid
trade to earn a pittance with, traced in delicate
letters by a hand the trapper would have died
for. A good five hundred miles that trail ran
northward before it ended at the couch of
skins, in the great room of the great house,
in which the chief lay dying. And when the
trapper struck it he struck it as an eagle
strikes homeward toward the cradle crag of
his younglings, when talons are heavy and
daylight scant. He drew his line by the star
that never sets, and little turning did he make
for rivers, rapids, or tangled swamp; for mountain slope or briery windfall. He drew a trail

no man had ever trod—a blazeless[2] trail, unmarked by stroke of axe or cut of knife, by broken twig or sharpened rod, struck into mold or moss, and by its angle[3] telling whence came the trailer, whither went he, and how fast. From earliest dawn till night thickened the woods and massed the trees into a solid blackness, he hurried on, straight as a pigeon flies when homing, studying no sign for guidance, leaving none to tell that he had come and gone. He was at middle prime of life, tough and pliant as an ashen bough grown on hill, seasoned in hall, sweated and strung by constant exercise for highest action,

[2] In order to mark the direction of his course in trailing through the woods the trailer slashes with his axe or knife the bark of the trees he passes, by which signs he is able to retrace his course safely, or follow the same trail easily some future time. A blazed trail is one thus plainly marked. A blazeless trail is one on which the trailer has no marks or "blazes" to run by, but draws his line by other and occult signs, which tell him in what direction he is going and which are known only by those initiated in the mysteries of woodcraft.

[3] Certain tribes of Indians north of the St. Lawrence left accurate record of their rate of progress, and how far they had come by the length and angle of the slanted sticks they drove here and there into the ground as they sped on. The Nasquapees were best known as practicing this habit.

and now each muscle and sinew of his superb and superbly conditioned frame was taut with tension of a strong desire—to reach the bed-side of the dying chief before he died. For the message read: "Come to me quick, for I am alone with the terror of death. The chief is dying. At the pillar of white rock, on the lake, a canoe, with oars and paddle, will be waiting."

The trapper was clad in buckskin from cap to moccasins. His tunic, belted tight and fringeless, was opened widely at the throat for freest breathing. A pack, small, but rounded with strained fullness, was at his back. His horn and pouch were knotted to his side. In tightened belt was knife, and, trailing muzzle down and held reversed, a double rifle. Stripped was the man for speed, as when balanced on the issue of the race hang life and death. As some great ship, caught by some sudden gale off Anticosti or Dead Man's reef, and bare of sail, stripped to her spars, past battures hollow and hoarse-voiced as death and ghastly white, and through the damned eddies that would suck her down and crush her with stones which grind forever and never see the light, sharpening their cuttings with their horrid grists, runs scudding; so ran the strong man northward, urged by a fear stronger than that of wreck on the ghost-peopled shore of deadly St. Lawrence. A hound, huge of size, bred to a hair, ambled steadily on at heel. And though he crossed many a hot scent, and more than once his hurrying master started a buck warm from his nest, and nose was busy with knowledge of game afoot, he gave no whimper nor swerved aside, but, silent, followed on in the swift way his master was so hurriedly making, as if he, too, felt the solemn need which urged the trail northward. Never before had runner faced a longer or a harder trail, or under high command or deadly peril pushed it so fiercely forward.

Seven days the trail ran thus, and still the man, tireless of foot, hurried on, and the hound followed silently at heel. What a body was his! How its powers responded to the soul's summons! For on this seventh day of highest effort, taxing with heavy strain each muscle, bone, and joint to the utmost, days lengthened from earliest dawn to deepest gloaming, the strong man's face was fresh, his eye was bright, and he swung steadily onward, with long, swinging, easy-motioned gait, as if the prolonged and terrible effort he was making was but a morning's burst of speed for healthy exercise.

The climate favored him. October, with all its glorious colors, was on the woods, and the warm body of the air was charged through and through with cool atmospheric movements from the north. It was an air to race for one's life in. Soft to the lungs, but filled to its blue edge with oxygen and that mystic element men call ozone; the overflow of God's vitality spilled over the azure brim of heaven, whose volatile flavor fills the nose of him who breathes the air of mountains. Favored thus by rare conditions, the best that nature gives the trailer, the strong man raced onward through the ripe woods like an old-time runner running for the laurel crown and the applause of Greece.

It was nigh sunset of the seventh day, and the trapper halted beside a spring, which bubbled coldly up from a cleft rock at the base of a cliff. He cast aside his hunting shirt, baring his body to the waist, and bathed himself in the cool water. He knelt to its mossy rim and sank his head slowly down into the refreshing depths, and held it there, that he might feel the delicious coolness run thrilling through his heated body. He cast his moccasins aside and bathed his feet, sore and hot from monstrous effort, sinking them knee deep in the cold flowage of the blessed spring. Then, refreshed, he stood upon the velvet bank, his mighty chest and back pink as a lady's palm, his strong feet glowing, his face aflush through its deep tan, while the wind dried him, and the golden leaves of the overhanging maples fell round him in showers.

Refreshed and strengthened, he reclothed himself, relaced his moccasins and tightened belt, but before he broke away he drew the

sheet of birchbark from his breast and read the
lines traced delicately thereon.

"Yes, I read aright," he muttered to himself; "the writing on the birch is plain as
ivy on the oak, and it says: 'Come to me
quick, for I am alone with the terror of death.
The chief lies dying. At the pillar of white
rock, on the lake, a canoe, with oars and paddle, will be waiting.'" And the trapper thrust
back the writing to its place above his heart
and burst away down the decline that lead to
the lake at a run.

"I've bent the trail like a fool," he muttered, as he reached the bottom of the dip,
"or the lake lies hereaway," and even as he
spoke the waters of a lake, red with the red
flame of the setting sun, gleamed like a field
of fire through the maple trees. The trapper
dashed a hand upward with a gesture of de-
light, and burst away again at a lope through
the russet bushes and golden leaves that lay
like plucked plumage, ankle deep, upon the
ground, toward the lake, burning redly
through the trees not fifty rods beyond. A

moment brought him to the shore, bordered
thick with cedar growths, and, breaking
through the fragrant branches with a leap,
he landed on a beach of silver sand, and lo!
to the left, not a dozen rods away, washed by
the red waves, stood the signal rock, fifty feet
in height, and from water line to summit
white as drifted snow.

"God be praised!" exclaimed the trapper,
and he lifted his cap reverently. "God be
praised that I reckoned the course aright and
ran the trail straight from end to end. For
the woods be wide and long, and to have
missed this lake would have been a sorry hap
when one like her is alone with the dying.
But where is the canoe that she said should
be here, for sixty miles of water cannot be
jumped like a brook or forded like a rapid,
and the island lies nigh the western shore,
and who may reach it afoot? And he ran his
eyes along the sand for signs to tell if boat
or human foot had pressed it.

He searched the beach a mile around the
bay, but not a sign of human presence could

be found. Then nigh the signal rock he sat upon the sand, unloosed his pack, and from it took crust and meat, of which he ate, then fed the hound, sharing the scant supper with him equally. "It is the last morsel, Rover," said the trapper to the dog as he fed him. "It is the last morsel in the pack, and you and I will breakfast lightly unless luck comes." The dog surely understood the master's saying, for he rolled his hungry eyes toward the pack as if he bitterly sensed the bitter prophecy; then—true canine philosopher as he was—he curled himself in a bunch of dried leaves contentedly, as if by extra sleep he would make good the lack of food.

"Thou art wiser than men!" exclaimed the trapper, looking reflectively at his canine companion, now snoring in his warm russet bed. "Thou art wiser, my dog, than men, for they waste breath and time in bewailing their hard fortunes, but you make good the loss that pinches thee by holding fast and quickly to the nearest gain." And he gazed upon the sleeping hound with reflecting and admiring eyes.

Then slowly behind the western hills sank
the red sun. The fervor faded from the water
and the lake darkened. The winds died with
the day. Gradually the farther shore retired
from sight, and the distinguishing hills became blankly black. The upper air held on
to the retreating light awhile, but finally sur-
rendered the last trace, and night held all the
world.

Amid the gathering gloom upon the beach
the trapper sat in counsel with his thoughts.
At length he rose, and with dry driftage within
reach kindled a fire. By the light of it he
cut some branches of nigh cedars, and with
them made a bed upon the sand, then cast
himself upon his fragrant couch. Twice he
rose and listened. Twice renewed the fire
with larger sticks. At last, tired nature failed
the will. The toil of the long trail fell
heavily on him. Slumber captured his senses
and he slept the sleep of sheer exhaustion.
But before he slept he muttered to himself:

"She said a canoe, with oars and paddle,
should be here, and the canoe will come."

The hours passed on. The Dipper turned its circle in the northern sky, and stars rose and set. The warm shores felt the coolness of the night, and from the water's edge a soft mist flowed and floated in thin layers along the cooling sands. The logs of seasoned woods glowed with a steady warmth in the calm air. The fog turned yellow as it drifted over the burning brands, so that a halo crowned the ruddy heat. The night was at its middle watch, when the hound rose to his feet and questioned the lake with lifted nose, but his mouth gave no signal. If one was coming, it was the coming of a friend. Ten minutes passed, then he whined softly, and, walking to the water's edge, waited expectant; not long, for in a moment a canoe, moving silently, as if wind-blown, came floating toward the beach, and lodged upon it noise-lessly, as bird on bough. And a girl, paddle in hand, stepped to his side, and, stooping, caressed his head, then moved toward the fire and stood above the sleeping man.

She gently stirred the brands until they

flamed, and in the light thus made studied the strong face, bronzed with the tan of the woods, the face of one who never failed friend nor fought foe in vain, and who had come so far and swiftly in answer to her call. She was of that old race who lived in the morning of the world, when giants walked the earth[4] and the sons of God married the daughters of men.[5] And the old blood's love of strength was in her. She noted the power and symmetry of his mighty frame, which lay relaxed from tension in the graceful attitude of sleep; the massive chest, broad as two common men's, which rose and fell to his deep breathing; the great, strongly corded neck, rooted to the vast trunk as some huge oak grown on a rounded hill. She noted, too, the large and shapely head, the thick, black hair, closely cropped, and the sleeper's face—where might woman find another like it?—lean of flesh,

[4] There were giants in the earth in those days. Gen. vi, 4.

[5] The sons of God saw the daughters of men that they were fair; and they took them wives of all which they chose. Gen. vi, 2.

large featured, plain, but stamped with the seal of honesty, chiseled clean of surplus by noble abstinence, and bearing on its front the look of pride, of power and courage to face foe or fate. Thus the girl sat and watched him as he slept, stirring the brands softly that she might not lose sight of a face which was to her the face of a god—such god as the proudest woman of her race, in the old time might, with art or goodness, have won and wedded.

Dawn came at last. The blue above turned gray. The stars shortened their pointed fires and faded. The east kindled and flamed. Heat flowed westward like an essential oil hidden in the pores and channels of the air; while light, brightly clean and clear, ran round the horizons, revealing its own and the loveliness of the world.

Then woke the birds. Morning found a voice sweet as her face. A hermit thrush sent her soft, pure call from the damp depths of the dripping woods. A woodpecker signaled breakfast with his hammer so sturdily that all the elfin echoes of the hills merrily mimiced him. An eagle, hunting through the sky, at the height of a mile, dropped like a plummet into the lake, and, struggling upward from his perilous plunge, heavily weighted, lined his slow flight straight toward his distant crag. The girl rose to her feet, and, leaning on her paddle, for a moment gazed long and tenderly at the sleeper's face, then softly breathed, " John Norton!"

The call, low as it was, broke through the leaden gates of slumber with the suddenness and effect of a great surprise. Quick as a flash he came to his feet, and, for a moment stood dazed, bewildered, his bodily powers breaking out of sleep quicker than his senses, and he saw the girl as visitant in vision. He stepped to the water's edge and bathed his face, and turning, freshened and fully awake, saw with glad and apprehensive eyes, who stood before him, and tenderly said :

" Is the da   ter of the old race well ?"

" Well, well I am, John Norton," answered

the girl, and her voice was low and softly musical, as water falling into water. "I am well, friend of my mother and my friend. And the chief still lives, and will live till you come, for so he bade me tell you." And she reached her small hand out to him. He took it in his own, and held it as one holds the hand of child, and answered :

"I am glad. Thou comest like a bird in the night, silently. Why did you not awake me when you came ?"

"Why should I wake thee, John Norton ?" returned the girl. "I am a day ahead of that the chief set for your coming. For our run- ner—the swiftest in the woods from Mistas- sinni to Labrador—said : 'Twelve suns must rise and set before my words could reach thee,' and the chief declared : 'No living man, not even you, could fetch the trail short of ten days.' He timed me to this rock himself, and told me when I would come nor wait another hour, that I would wait by the white rock two days before I saw your face. But I would come, for a voice within me said—a voice which runs vocal in our blood, and has so run through all my race since the beginning of the world—this voice within kept saying: ' *Go, for thou shalt find him there !*' And so I, hurrying, came. But tell me how many days were you upon the trail ?"

" I fetched the trail in seven days from sun to sun," answered the trapper, modestly.

" Seven days !" exclaimed the girl, while the light of a great surprise and admiration shone in her eyes. " Seven days ! Thou hast the deer's foot and the cougar's strength, John Norton. No wonder that the war chiefs love you."

And then after a moment's pause :

" But why didst thou push the trail so fiercely ?"

" I read your summons and I came," replied the trapper, sententiously.

The girl started at the hearing of the words, which told her so simply of her power over the man in front of her. Her nostrils dilated, and through the glorious swarth of her cheek there came a flash of deeper red. The gloom

of her eyes moistened like glass to the breath.
Her ripe lips parted as to the passing of a
gasp, and the full form lifted as if the spirit
of passion within would fling the beautiful
frame it filled upon the strong man's bosom.
Thus a moment the sweet whirlwind seized
and shook her, then passed. Her eyes drooped
modestly, and with a sweet humbleness, as
one who has received from heaven beyond her
hope or merit, she simply said:

"I have brought you food, John Norton.
Come and eat."

The food was of the woods. Bread coarse and
brown, but sweet with the full cereal sweetness; corn, parched in the fire, which eaten,
lingered long as a rich flavor in the mouth;
venison, roasted for a hunter's hunger, within
whose crisp surface the life of the deer still
showed redly; water from the lake, drank
from a cup shaped from the inner bark of the
golden birch, whose hollow curvature still
burned with warm chrome colors. So, on the
cool lake shore, in the red light of early morn,
they broke their fast.

The trapper ate as a strong man eats after long toil and scant feeding, not grossly, but with a heartiness good to see. The girl ate little, and that absently, as if the atoms in her mouth were foreign to her senses and no taste followed eating.

" You do not eat," said the trapper. " The sun will darken on the lower hills before we come to food again. Are you not hungry?"

" Last night I was ahungered," answered the girl, musingly. " But now I hunger no more," and her face was as the face of a Madonna holding her child, full of a plentiful and sweet content.

" I do not understand you," returned the trapper, after a moment's silence. " Your words be plain, but their sense is hidden. Why are you not hungry?"

" You read me once out of your sacred books, John Norton, that man does not live by bread alone, but by every word that proceedeth out of the mouth," responded the girl. " I knew not then the meaning of the words, for I was a girl, and had no understanding,

and the words were old, older than your books,
and therefore deeply wise, and I, being young,
did not know. But I know now." And here
the girl paused a moment, hesitated as a young
bird to leave the sure bough for the first time,
then, rallying courage for the deed, gazed with
her large eyes lovingly into his, and timidly
explained:

"I am not hungry, John Norton, for God
has fed me!"

To the tanned cheek of the trapper there
rushed a glow like the flush to the face of a
girl. The light of a happy astonishment
leaped from his eyes, and his breath came
strongly. Then light and color faded, and as
one vexed and heartily ashamed of his vanity,
while the lines of his face tightened, he made
harsh answer:

"Talk no more in riddles, lest I be a fool
and read the riddle awry. Nor jest again on
matters grave as life, lest I, who am but
mortal man and slow withal, forget wisdom
and take thy girlish playfulness for earnest
talk. Nay, nay," he added earnestly, as she

rose to her feet with an exclamation of passionate pain, " Say not another word, you have
done no ill. You be young and fanciful, and
I—I be a fool! Come, let us go. The pull
is long, and we will need the full day's light
to reach the island ere night falls." And,
placing his rifle in the canoe, he signaled to
the hound and seated himself at the oars.
The girl obeyed his word, stepped to her place
and pushed the light boat from the sands on
which so much had been received and so much
missed. Perhaps her woman's heart foretold
her that love like hers would get, even as it
gave, all at last.

*   *   *   *   *   *   *   *

The house was large and lofty, builded of
logs squared smoothly and mortared neatly
between the edges. In the thick walls were
deep embrasures, that light through the great
windows might be more abundant. The
builders loved the sun and made wide path-
ways for its entrance everywhere. The case-
ments, fashioned to receive storm shutters,
were proof against winter's wind and lead

alike. In the steep roof were dormer windows, glassed with panes, tightly soldered to
the sash. At either end of the great house a
huge chimney rose, whose solid masonry of
stone stood boldly out from the hewn logs,
framed closely against its mortared sides. A
wide veranda ran the entire length of the
southern side. A balustrade of cedar logs,
each hewn until it showed its red and fragrant
heart, ran completely round it. Above posts
of the same sweetly odored wood—whose fragrance, with its substance, lasts forever—was
lattice work of poles stripped of their birchen
bark and snowy white, on which a huge vine
ran its brown tracery, enriched with bunches,
heavily pendent, of blue black grapes—that
pungent growth of northern woods, whose
odors make the winding rivers sweet as
heaven. In front, a natural lawn sloped to
the yellow sands, on which the waves fell
with soft sound.

Eastward, a widely acred field, showed care-
ful husbandry. Garnet and yellow colored
pods hung gracefully from the brown poles.

The ripened corn showed golden through the parted husks, and beds of red and yellow beets patched the dark soil with their high colors. The solar flower turned its broad disk toward the wheeling sun, while dahlias, marigold, and hardy annuals, with their bright colors, warmed like a floral campfire the stretch of gray stubble and pale barren beyond. It was a lovely and a lonely spot, graced by a lordly home, such as the wealthy worthies builded here and there in the great wilderness for comfort and for safety in the old savage days when feudal lords [6] made good their claim to forest seigniories with sword and musket, and every house was home and castle.

The canoe ran lightly shoreward. The beach received its pressure as a mother's bosom receives the child running from afar to its reception—yieldingly ; and on the welcoming sand the light bark rested. The trapper stepped

[6] The reader will recall that old Canada, viz., the Province of Quebec was wholly French in origin, and that its organization rested on the feudal basis, the whole territory occupied being divided not into towns and counties, but into seigniories.

ashore and reached his hand back to the girl. Her velvet palm touched his, rough and strong, as thistledown, wind blown, the oak tree's bark, then nestled and stayed. Thus the two stood hand in hand, gazing up the sloping lawn at the great house, the broad, bright field and the circling forest, glowing with autumnal colors, which made the glorious background. The green lawn, the great gray house, and the vast woods belting it around, brightly beautiful, made such a landscape picture as Titian would have reveled in. It stood, this mansion of the woods, this wilderness castle, in glorious loneliness, a part and centre of a splendid solitude, beyond the coming and going of men, beyond their wars and peace, the creation and embodiment of a mystery deep as the woods around it; a strange, astounding spectacle to one who did not know the history of the forest.

" It is a noble place," exclaimed the trapper, as he gazed up the wide lawn at the great house, and swept with admiring glance the glorious circle of the woods which curved their belt of splendor round it ; " it is a noble place, and if mortal man might find content on earth, he might find it here."

" Could you, John Norton, living here, be content ?" inquired the girl, and she lifted the splendor of her eyes to his strong, honest face.

" Content," returned the trapper, innocently, " why, what more could mortal crave than is here to his hand ? A field to give him bread, a noble house to live in, the waters full of fish, the woods of game, the sugar of the maple for his sweetening, honey for his feasts, and not a trap within two hundred miles. What more could mortal man, of good judgment, crave ?"

" Is there nothing else, John Norton ?" asked the girl.

" Aye, aye," returned the trapper, " one thing. I did forget the dog. A hunter should have his hound."

A shade of pain, perhaps vexation, came to her face as she heard the trapper's answer. She withdrew her hand from his and said : " Food, fur, and a house are not enough, John Norton. A dog is good for camp and trail. Sol-

itude is sweet and the absence of wicked **men**
a boon. But these do not make home nor
heaven, both of which we crave and both of
which are possible on earth, for the conditions
are possible. The chief has found this spot a
dreary place since mother died."

"Your mother was an angel," answered the
trapper, " and your words are those of wisdom.
I have thought at times of the things you hint
at, and, as a boy, I had vain dreams, for nature
is nature. But I have my ideas of woman and
I love perfect things. And I—I am but a
.hunter, an unlearned man, without education,
or house, or land, or gold, and I am not fit for
any woman that is fit for me!"

The change that came to the girl's face at
the trapper's words—for he had spoken gravely,
and through the honesty of his speech she
looked and saw the greatness and humility of
his nature—was one to be to him who saw it
a memory forever. The shadow left it and its
dusky splendor was lighted with the glow of
a blessed assurance. This man would love
her! This man with the eagle's eye, the

deer's foot, the cougar's strength, the honest heart, would love her! This man her mother reverenced, her uncle loved, who twice had saved her life at the risk of his, whose skill and courage were the talk of a thousand camps, whose simple word in pledge held faster than other's oaths—this man into whose very bosom her soul had looked as into a clean place—this man would love her! If heaven be what good men say, and all its bliss had been pledged to her when she lay dying, her body would not have thrilled with a warmer glow than rushed its sweet heat through her veins at that instant of blessed conviction. Wait! She could wait for years, but she would win him—win him to herself; win him from his blindness, which did him honor, to that dazzling light in whose glory man stands but once; but, standing so, sees, with a glad bewilderment, that the woman he dares not love, because she is so infinitely better than he, loves him! Yes, she would win him—win him with such sweet art, such patient approaches, such seductiveness of innocent passion, slowly and deliciously disclosed, that he should never know of his temerity until, thus drawn to her, she held him in her arms irrevocably, in bonds that only cold and hateful death could part. Through all her leaping blood this blessed hope, this sure, sweet knowledge flowed like spiced wine. This man, this man she worshiped, he would love her! It was enough. Her cup ran full to the brim and overflowed. She simply took the trapper's hand again and said:

"We will go to the chamber of the chief. His eyes will brighten when he sees thy face."

CHAPTER II.

THE FIGHT AT MAMELONS.[7]

"IT was a dreadful fight, John Norton. We went into it a thousand warriors on a side, and in either army were twenty chiefs of fame. We fought the fight at Mamelons, where, at sunset, we met the Esquimaux,[8] coming up as we were going down. The Montaignais headed the war. The Mountaineers,[9] whose fathers' wigwams stood at Mamelons, had fought the Esquimaux a thousand years, and both had wrongs to right. My father died that summer, and I, fresh

---

[7] This old battle-ground is located on the high terraces which define the several sand mounds now standing back of Tadousac.

[8] The Esquimaux were numerous and very warlike, and at one time had pushed their conquests clean up to the Saguenay.

[9] The Montagnais Indians held the country, from Quebec down to the Esquimaux, near Seven Islands, and called themselves "Mountaineers."

31

from the fields of France, headed my tribe.
You know how small it was, the last remnant
of the old Lenape root, but every man a warrior. I knew not the right or wrong of it,
nor did I care. I only knew our tribe was
pledged to the Nasquapees[10] of frozen Ungava,
and they were allies of the Mountaineers, and
hence the fight held us to its edge. That
night we slept under truce, but when the sun
came up went at it. I see that morning now.
The sun from out the eastern sea rose red as
blood. The Nasquapees, who lived as athe-

---

[10] The Nasquapees are one of the most remarkable families of Indians on the continent, and of whom but little is
known. Their country extends from Lake Mistassinni
eastward to Labrador, and from Ungava Bay to the coast
mountains of the St. Lawrence. They are small in size,
fine featured, with mild, dark eyes, and extremely small
hands and feet. The name Nasquapees—Nasqupics—
means "a people who stand straight." They have no
Medicine man or prophet, and hence are called by other
tribes atheists. Their sense of smell is so acute that it
rivals the dog's. "Spirit rappings," and other strange
manifestations, peculiar to us moderns, have been prac-
ticed immemorially among them and carried to such a shade
of success that one of our Boston seances would be a laughable and bungling affair to them. Their language is like
the Western Crees, and their traditions point to a remote
eastern origin.

ists without a Medicine man, cared not for this, but the prophet of the Mountaineers painted his face and body black as night, tore his blanket into shreds, and lay in the sand as one dead. The Nasquapees laughed, but we of the mountains knew by that dread sign that our faces looked toward our last battle. We made it a brave doom. We fought till noon upon the shifting sands, nor gained an inch, nor did our foes, when suddenly the sun was clouded and a great wind arose that drove the sand so thickly that it hid the battle. The firing and the shouting ceased along the terrace where we fought, and a great, dread silence fell on the mighty mounds, save when the fierce gusts smote them. Thus, living and dead, friend and foe, we lay together, our faces plunged into the coarse gravel, our hands clutching the rounded stones, that we might breathe and stay until the wind might pass. And such a wind was never blown on man before, for it was hot and came straight down from heaven, so that our backs winced as we lay flattened. Thus, mixed and mingled, we clung to the hot stones, while some crept in beneath the dead for shelter. So both wars clung to the ground for an hour's space. Then, suddenly, the sun rushed out, and shaking sand from eyes and hair, and spitting it from our mouths, at it we went again. It was an awful fight, John Norton, and more than once, in the mad midst of it, smoke-blinded and sand-choked, I thought of you and that I heard your rifle crack."

"I would to God I had been there!" exclaimed the trapper, and he dashed his huge hand into the air, as if cheering a line of battle on, while his eyes blazed and his face whitened.

"I would to God you had been!" returned the chief. "For whether one lived through it, or died in it, we made it great by great fighting. For we fought it to the end in spite of interruptions."

"Interruptions!" exclaimed the trapper. "I do not understand ye, chief. What but death could interrupt a fight like that?"

"Listen, trapper listen," rejoined the chief,

excitedly. " Listen, that you may understand what stopped the fight, for never since man was born was fought such fight as we fought, high up above the sea, that day at Mamelons. I told you it was an old feud between the Mountaineers and Esquimaux, a feud that had held its heat hot for a thousand years, and we, a thousand on each side, one for each year, fought on the sand, while above, below, and around the dead of a thousand years, slain in the feud, fought too."

" Nay, nay," exclaimed the trapper. " Chief, it cannot be. The dead fight not, but live in peace forever, praise be to God," and he bowed his head reverently.

" That is your faith, not mine, John Norton, for I hold to an older faith—that men by a knife's thrust are not changed, but go, with all their passions with them, to the Spirit Land, and there build upward on the old foundation. And so, I say again, that the dead of a thousand years fought in the air above and around us on that day at Mamelons. For, in the pauses of the wind, we who fought on either side heard shrieks, and shouts, and tramplings as of ten thousand feet, and over us were roarings, and bellowings, and hollow noises, dreadful to hear, and through all the battle went the word that '*the old dead were fighting, too!*' and that made us wild. Both sides went mad. The dying cheered the living, and the living cheered the dead. So went the battle—the fathers and the sons, the dead and living, hard at it. The waters of the Saguenay, a thousand feet below, were beaten into foam by the rush of fighting feet, and the roaring of a great battle filled its mouth. Its dark tide whitened with strange death froth from shore to shore, while ever and anon its surface shivered and shook. And under us on the high crest, cloud-wrapped, the earth trembled as we fought, so that more than once as we stood clinched, we two, the foe and I, still gripped for death, would pause until the ground grew steady, for its tremblings made us dizzy, then clinch the fiercer, mad with a great madness at being stopped in such death-grapple. Under us all

the long afternoon the great mounds rose and
sank like waves that have no base to stand
upon. The clouds snowed ashes. Mud fell
in showers. The air we breathed stank with
brimestone and burnt bones. And still it
thickened, and still both sides, now but a
scattered few, fought on, until at last, with a
crash, as if the world had split apart, darkness, deep as death, fell suddenly, so that eyes
were vain, and we who were not dead, unable
to find foe, stood still. And thus the battle
ended, even drawn, because God stopped the
fight at Mamelons.[11]

✻ ✻ ✻ ✻ ✻ ✻ ✻ ✻

[11] The Saguenay is undoubtedly of earthquake origin.
The north shore of the St. Lawrence from Cape Tourmente
to Point du Monts, is one of the earthquake centres of the
world. In 1663 a frightful series of convulsions occurred,
lasting for more than four months; and, it is said, that not
a year passes that motions are not felt in the earth. The
old maelstrom at Bai St. Paul was caused by subterranean
force, and by subsequent shocks deprived of its terrible
power. The mouth of the Saguenay was one of the great
rendezvous of the Indian races long before Jacques Cartier
came, and the great mounds above Tadousac have been
the scene of many great Indian battles ; but I would not
make affidavit that an earthquake ever did actually take
place while one was being fought, although there may have
been, and certainly, from an artistic point of view, there
should have been, such a poetic conjunction.

" At last the morning dawned at Mamelons, and never since those ancient beaches[12] saw the world's first morning, had the round sun looked down on such a scene. The great terraces on which we fought were ankle deep with ashes mixed with mud, and cinders black and hard, like burnt iron, and all the sand was soaked with blood. The dead were heaped. They lay like drifted wreckage on a beach, where the eddying surges of the battle tossed them in piles and tangled heaps like jammed timber. For in the darkness, we had fought by sound, and not by sight, and where the battle roared loudest, thither had we rushed, using axe and knife and the short seal spears of the damned Esquimaux. And all the later battle was fought breast to breast, for ere half were dead, powder and lead gave out, and the fray was

[12] These mamelons, or great sand mounds, are believed to be the old geologic beaches of earliest times. They rise in tiers, or great terraces, one above the other, to a great height, the uppermost one being a thousand feet or more above the Saguenay, and represent, as they run down from terrace to terrace, the shrinking of the " face of the deep" in the creative period, by the shrinking of which the solid earth rose in sight.

hand to hand, until, by the sickening darkness, God stopped it.

" I searched the dreadful field from end to
end to find my own, and found them. With
blackened hands, clouted with blood, I drew
them together. Forty in all, I stretched them,
side by side, and the savage pride of the old
blood in me burst from my mouth in a shrill
yell, when I saw that twenty swarthy bosoms
showed the knife's thrust deep and wide. They
died like warriors, trapper, true to the old Lenape blood, whose Tortoise[13] steadfastness upheld the world. I made a mound above their
bodies, and heaped it high with rounded stones
which crowned the uppermost beach, and made

[13] The Lenni-Lenape had, at the coming of the whites,
their territory on the Delaware, but their traditions point to
long journeyings from the east over wide waters and cold
countries. Their language, strange to say, has in it words
identical with the old Basque tongue, and establishes some
community of origin or history in the remote ages. The
Lenni-Lenape had as their Totem, or sacred sign of origin
and blood, a Tortoise with a globe on its back, and boasted
that they were the oldest of all races of men, tracing their
descent through the ages to that day when the world
was upheld by a Tortoise, or turtle, resting in the midst of
the waters. As a tribe they were very brave, proud, and
honorable.

wail above friends and kindred fallen in strange feud. And there they sleep, on that high verge, where the unwritten knowledge of my fathers, told from age to age, declare the waters of the earliest morning first found shore." [See note 12.]

"Never did I hear a tale like this," exclaimed the trapper. "Strange stories of this fight I heard in the far north, chanted in darkness at midnight, with wild wailing of the tribes ; but I held it as the trick of sorcerers to frighten with. Go on and tell me all. Chief, what next befell thee ?"

"John Norton, thou hast come half a thousand miles to hear a tale of death told by a dying man. Listen, and remember all I say, for at the close it touches close on thee. A fate whose meshes woven when our blood was crossed has tangled all that bore our name in ruin from the start, and with my going only one remains to suffer further."

Here the chief paused while one might count a score, then, looking steadily at the trapper, said :

" Last month, when the raven was on the moon,[14] my warning came. The old wound opened without cause, and, lying on this bed, I saw the hour of my death, and beyond, thee, I saw, and beside thee the last and sweetest of our line, and the same doom was over her as has been to us all since the fatal cross—the doom which sends courage and beauty to a quick, sad death."

" I do not understand," replied the trapper. " Tell me what befell thee further, step by step, and how I, a man without a cross,[15] can be connected with the old traditions of thy tribe and house ?"

" Listen. In coming from the field, I saw, half-covered by the ashes, a body clothed in a foreign garb. It lay face downward where the dead were thickest, one arm outstretched, the hand of which, gloved to the wrist, still gripped a sword, red to its jeweled hilt. The head was foul with ash and sand, but I noted that

[14] When the raven was on the moon. An Indian description of an eclipse.

[15] A man without a cross, viz., a pure-blooded man. A white man without any Indian or foreign blood in his veins.

the hair was black and long, and worn like a
warrior's of our ancient race. Then I remem-
bered a habit of boyish days and pride. Trembling, I stooped, lifted the body upward and
turned the dead face toward me. And there,
there on that field of Mamelons, where it was
said of old, before one of my blood had ever
seen the salted shore, the last of our race
should die, all foul with ash and sand and
blood, brows knit with battle rage, teeth bared
and tightly set, *I saw my brother's face!*"

"God in heaven!" exclaimed the trapper.
" How came he there, and who killed him?"

" John Norton, you know our cross, and that
the best blood of the old world and the new,
older than the old, is in our veins. My grand-
sire was the son of one who stood next to the
throne of France, and all our line have studied
in her polished schools since red and white
blood mingled in our veins. There did we
two, my brother and I, remain until my father
called us home. I left him high in the court's
favor. Thence, suddenly, without sending
word, with a young wife and office of trust, he

voyaged, hoping to give me glad surprise. A
tempest drove his ship on Labrador; but he
saved wife and gold. The Esquimaux proved
friendly, and gave him help, and, reckless of
consequence, as have been all our line since
the French taint came to us, not knowing
cause, he joined the wild horde, and came with
them to fatal Mamelons and its dread fight.

"So chanced it, trapper. I dropped the body
from my arms, for a great sickness seized me
and my head swam, and in the bloody tangle
of dead bodies I sat limp and lifeless. Then
in a frenzy, clutching madly at a straw of
hope, I tore the waistcoat, corded with gold,
from the stiff breast to find proof that would
not lie. And there, there above his heart, with
eyes bloodshot and bulging, I saw the emblem
of our tribe—the Tortoise, with the round
world on his back; and through the sacred
Totem of our ancient lineage, which our father's
hand had tattooed on his chest and mine; yea,
through it and the white skin above his heart,
there gaped a gash, swollen and red, which my
own knife had made. For in the darkness of

the fight, bearing up against an Esquimaux
rush, ash blinded, I found a foe who swore in
French and had a sword. He and I fought
grappling in the dark, when the earth hove
beneath our feet and ashes rained upon us;
and his sword ran me through even as I thrust
my long knife into him.

"And thus at Mamelons, where sits the doom
of our race awaiting us, in its dread fight,
both fighting without cause, I slew my
brother, and from his hand I got the wound
from whose old poison I now die.

"Thus I stood among the dead at Mamelons, a chief without a tribe and my brother's
murderer. I moved some bodies and scraped
downward, that I might have clean sand to
fall upon; then drew my knife to let life out,
and thus meet bravely the old doom foretold
for me and mine as awaiting us since man
was born on the shore of that first world.
But even as I bent to the knife's point, a
voice called me and I turned.

"It was an Esquimau; the only chief left
from the fight; my brother's host seeking my

brother. He knew me, for he and I had clinched in the great fight, but the earth opening parted us, and so both lived. Each felt for each as warriors feel for a brave foe when the red fight is ended and the field of death is heavy. Thus, battle tired, amid the dead, we lifted hands, palm outward, and met in peace. He knew the language of old France, and I told him of my woe, of our old race, of tribesmen dead, of brother slain by my own hand, and of the doom that waited for us over Mamelons. And then he spoke and told me what stayed my hand and held me unto further life.

"Seven days I journeyed with him, and on the eighth came to where she sat, amid his children, in his rude house at Labrador. Never, since God created woman, was one made so beautiful as she. She was of that old Iberian race, whose birth is older than annals, whose men conquered the world and whose women wedded gods. She was a Basque,[16] and her ancestor's ships had an-

[16] As far back in time as annals or tradition extend, a race of men called Iberians dwelt on the Spanish peninsula.

chored under Mamelons a thousand years
before the Breton came. Fresh from the
dreadful field, with heart of lead, my brother's

Winchell says that "these Iberians spread over Spain,
Gaul, and the British Islands as early as 5000 B. C. When
Egypt was only at her fourth dynasty this race had con-
quered all the world west of the Mediterranean."

They originally settled Sardinia, Italy, and Sicily, and
spread northward as far as Norway and Sweden. Strabo
says, speaking of a branch of this race : "They employ the
art of writing, and have written books containing memo-
rials of ancient times, and also poems and laws set in verse,
for which they claim an antiquity of 6000 years. These
old Iberians to-day are represented by the Basques. The
Basques are fast dying out, and but a small remnant is
left. They undoubtedly represent the first race of men.
They are **proud**, merry, and passionate. The women are
very beautiful, and noted for their wit, vivacity, and subtle
grace of person. They love music, and dance much.
Some of their dances are symbolic and connected with
their ancient mysteries. Their language is unconnected
with any European tongue or dialect, but, strange to say,
it is connected by close resemblance, in many words, with
the Maiya language of Central America and that of the
Algolquin-Lenape and a few other of our Indian tribes.
Duponceau says of the Basque tongue :

"This language, preserved in a corner of Europe by a
few thousand Mountaineers, is the sole remaining fragment
of perhaps a hundred dialects, constructed on the same
plan, which probably existed and were universally spoken
at a remote period in that quarter of the world. Like the
bones of the mammoth, it remains a monument of the
destruction produced by a succession of ages. It stands
single and alone of its kind, surrounded by idioms that
have no affinity with it."

face staring whitely at me as I talked, I told her all—the fight, the death of brother and of tribe, and the doom that waited for our blood above the shining sands at Mamelons.

"She listened to the end. Then rose and took my hand and kissed it, saying : ' Brother, I kiss thy hand as head of our house. What's done is done. The dead cannot come back.' Then, covering up her face with her rich laces, she went within the hanging skins, and for seven days was hidden with her woe.

"But when the seven days were passed she came, and we held council. Next morn, with ten canoes deep laden with gold and precious stuffs, that portion of her dower saved from the wreck, we started hitherward. This island, after many days of voyaging, we reached, and here we landed, by chance or fate I know not, for she spake the word that stopped us here, not I. For on this island did my fathers live, and here the fateful cross came to our blood, that cross with France which was not fit; for the traditions of our tribe—a mystery for a thousand years—had said that any cross of red

with white should ripen doom at Mamelons;
for there the white first landed on the shore of
this western world.[17]

"She needed refuge, for within her life another life was growing. Brooding, she prayed
that the new soul within her might not be a
boy. 'A boy,' she said, 'must meet the doom
foretold. A girl, perchance, might not be
held.' Her faith and mine were one, save hers
was older, she being of the old trunk stock, of
which the world-supporting Tortoise were a

[17] The antiquity of European visitation to the St. Lawrence is unascertained, and, perhaps, unascertainable. But
there is good reason to think that long before Jacques Cartier, Cabot, or even the Norsemen, ever saw the American
continent, the old Basque people carried on a regular commerce in fish and fur with the St. Lawrence. It is not
impossible but that Columbus obtained sure knowledge of
a western hemisphere from the old race, who dwelt, and
had dwelt, immemorially among the mountains of Spain,
as well as from the Norse charts. Their language, legends,
traditions and many signs compel one to the conclusion
that the old Iberian race, who once held all modern Europe
and the British isle in subjection, was of ocean origin, and
pushed on the van of an old-time and world-wide naviga-
tion beyond the record of modern annals. Both Jacques
Cartier and John Cabot found, with astonishment, old Basque
names everywhere, as they sailed up the coast, the date of
whose connection with the geography of the shores the natives could not tell.

branch; and so my blood was later, flowing from noonday fountains, while hers ran warm and red, a pure, sole stream, which burst from out the ponderous front of dead eternity, when, with His living rod, God smote it, in the red sunrise of the world. On this her soul was set, nor could I change her thought with reason, which I vainly tried, lest if the birth should prove a boy, the shock should kill her. But she held stoutly to it, saying:

" 'The women of our race get what they crave. My child shall be a woman, and being so, win what she plays for.'

" And, lo! she had her wish; for when the babe was born it was a girl.

" All since is known to you, for you, by a strange fate, blown, like a cone of the high pine from the midst of whirlwinds, when forest fires are kindled and the gales made by their heat blow hot a thousand miles across the land, dropped on this island like help from Heaven. Twice was I saved from death by thee. Twice was she rescued at the peril of thy life; mother and child, by thy quick

hand, snatched out of death. And when the
cursed fever came, and she and I lay, like two
burnt brands, you nursed us both, and from
your arms at last, her eyes upon you lovingly,
her soul unwillingly went from us. And her
sweet form, instinct with the old grace and
passion of that vanished race which once out-
rivaled Heaven's beauty and won wedlock with
the gods, lay on your bosom as some rare
rose, touched by untimely frost, while yet its
royal bloom is opening to the sun, lies, leaf
loosened, a lovely ruin rudely made on the
harsh gravel walk."

Here the chief stopped short, struck through
and through with sharp pains. His face whitened and he groaned. The spasm passed, but
left him weak. Rallying, with effort, he went
on :

"I must be brief. That spasm was the
second. The third will end me. God! How
the old stab jumps to-night!

"Trapper, you know how wide our titles •
reach. A hundred miles from east to west,
from north to south, the manor runs. It is a

princely stretch. A time will come when cities will be on it, and its deeds of warranty be worth a kingdom. Would that a boy outside the deadly limits of the cross, but dashed with the old blood in vein and skin, might be born to heir the place and live as master on these lakes and hills, where the great chiefs who bore the Tortoise sign upon their breasts when it upheld the world, beyond the years of mortal memory, lived and hunted! For when the doom in the far past, before one of our blood had ever seen the salted shore, was spoken, it was said:

"'This doom, for sin against the blood, shall not touch one born in the female line from sire without a cross.'

"I tell you, trapper, a thousand chiefs of the old race would leave their graves and fight again at Mamelons to see the old doom broken, and a boy, with one trace of red blood in vein and skin, ruling as master here! And I, who die to-night, I, and he who gave me death and whom I slew, would rise to lead them!

"John Norton, you I have called; you who

have saved my life and whose life I have saved;
you, who have stood in battle with me when
the line wavered and we two saved the fight;
you who have the wild deer's foot, the cougar's
strength, whose word once given stands, like
a chief's, the test of fire; you, all white in face,
all red at heart, a Tortoise, and yet a man
without a cross, have I called half a thousand
miles to ask with dying breath this question:

"May not that boy be born, the old race
kept alive, the long curse stayed, and ended
with my life forever be the doom of Mamelons?
Speak, trapper, friend, comrade in war, in
hunt and hall, speak to my failing ear, that I
may die exultant and tell the thousand chiefs
that throng to greet me in the spirit land that
the old doom is lifted and a race with blood of
theirs in vein and skin shall live and rule forever mid their native hills?"

From the first word the strange tale, half
chanted, had rolled on, like the great river flood-
ing upward from the gulf, between narrowing
banks, with swift and swifter motion, growing
pent and tremulous as it flows, until it chal-

lenges the base of Cape Tourment with thunder. And not until the dying chief, with headlong haste, had launched the query forth—the solemn query, whose answer would fix the bounds of fate forever—did the trapper dream whither the wild tale tended. His face whitened like a dead man's, and he stood dumb—dumb with doubt and fear and shame. At last, with effort, as when one lifts a mighty weight, he said, and the words were heaved from out his chest, as great weights from deep depths: "Chief, ye know not what ye ask. My God! I am not fit!"

Across the swarth face of the dying man there swept a flash of flame, and his glazed eyes lighted with a mighty joy.

"Enough! enough! It is enough!" he said. "The women of her race will have their way, and she will win thee. God! If I might live to see that brave boy born, the spent fountain of the old race filled again by that rich tide in her which flows red and warm from the sunrise of the world! Nay, nay. Answer me not. I leave it in the hands of

fate. Before I pass the seeing eye will come,
and I shall see if sunlight shines on Mamelons."

He touched a silver bell above his head,
and, after pause, the girl, in whom the beauty
of her mother and her race lived on, whose
form was lithe, but rounded full, whose face
was dark as woods, but warmly toned with
the old Basque splendor, like wine when light
shines through it, type of the two oldest and
handsomest races of the world, stood by his
side.

Long gazed the chief upon her, a vision too
beautiful for earth, too warm for heaven. The
light of a great pride was in his eyes, but
shaded with mournful pity.

"Last of my race," he murmured. "Last
of my blood, farewell! Thou hast thy mother's beauty, and not a trace of the damned
cross is on thee. Follow thou thy heart. The
women of thy race won so. My feet are on
the endless trail blazed by my fathers for ten
thousand years. I cannot tarry if I would.
I leave thee under care of this just man. Be

thou his comfort, as he will be thy shield. There is a chest, thy mother's dying gift, thou knowest where. Open and read, then shalt thou know. Trapper, read thou the ritual of the church above my bier. So shall it please thee. Thou art the only Christian I ever knew who kept his word and did not cheat the red man. Some trace of the old faiths, therefore, there must be in these modern creeds, albeit the holders of them cheat and fight each other. But, daughter of my house, last of my blood, born under shadow, and it may be unto doom, make thou my burial in the old fashion of thy race, older than mine. These modern creeds and mushroom rituals are not for us whose faiths were born when God was on the earth, and His sons married the daughters of men. So bury me, that I may join the old-time people who lived near neighbors to this modern God, and married their daughters to His sons."

Here paused he for a space, for the old wound jumped, and life flowed with his blood.

Then suddenly a change came to his face.

His eyes grew fixed. He placed one hand above them, as if to help them see afar. A moment thus. Then, whispering hoarsely, said:

"Take thou his hand. Cling to it. The old Tortoise sight at death is coming. I see the past and future. Daughter, I see thee now, and by thy side, thy arms around his neck, his arms round thee, the man without a cross! Aye. She was right. 'The women of my race get what they crave.' Girl, thou hast won! Rejoice, rejoice and sing. But, oh! my God! My God! John Norton! Look! Daughter, last of my blood, in spite of all, in spite of all, above thy head hangs, breaking black, the doom of Mamelons!"

And with these words of horror on his lips, the chief, whose bosom bore the Tortoise sign, who killed his brother under doom at Mamelons, fell back stone dead.

So died he. On the third day they built his bier in the great hall, and placed him on it, stripped like a warrior, to his waist, for so he charged the trapper it should be. Thus sitting in the great chair of cedar, hewn to the fragrant heart, in the wide hall, hound at feet, the Tortoise showing plainly on his breast, a fire of great knots, gummed with odorous pitch, blazing on the hearth, the two, each by the faith that guided, made, for the dead chief of a dead tribe, strange funeral.

And first, the trapper, standing by the bier, gazed long and steadfastly at the dead man's face. Then the girl, going to the mantel, reached for a book and placed it in his hand and stood beside him.

Then, after pause, he read:

" *I am the resurrection and the Life.*"

And the liturgy, voiced deeply and slowly read, as by one who readeth little and labors with the words, sounded through the great hall solemnly.

Then the girl, standing by his side, in the splendor of her beauty, the lights shining warmly on the dark glory of her face, lifted up her voice—a voice fugitive from heaven's choir —and sang the words the trapper had intoned:

" *I am the resurrection and the Life.*"

And her rich tones, pure as note of hermit
thrush cleaving the still air of forest swamps;
clear as the song of morning lark singing in
the dewy sky, rose to the hewn rafters and
swelled against the compressing roof. as if
they would break out of such imprisonment,
and roll their waves of sound afar and upward
until they mingled with kindred tones in
heaven.

Again the trapper:

"*He who believeth in me, though he were
dead, yet shall he live !*"

And again the marvelous voice pealed forth
the words of everlasting hope, as if from the
old race that lived in the dawn of the world,
whose blood was in her rich and red, had come
to her the memory of the music they had
heard run thrilling through the happy air
when the stars of the morning sang together for
joy.

Alas, that such a voice from the old days of
soul and song should lie smothered forever
beneath the sand of Mamelons!

Thus the first part. For the trapper, like

a Christian man without cross, would give his dead friend holy burial. Then came a pause. And for a space the two sat silent in the great hall, while the pitch knots flamed and flared their splashes of red light through the gloom.

Then rose the girl and took the trapper's place at the dead man's feet. Her hair, black with a glossy blackness, swept the floor. A jewel, large and lustrous, an heirloom of her mother's race, old as the world, burning with Atlantean flame, a miracle of stone-imprisoned fire, blazed on her brow. The large gloom of her eyes was turned upon the dead man's face, and the sadness of ten thousand years of life and loss was darkly orbed within their long and heavy lashes. Her small, swarth hands hung lifeless at her side, and the bowed contour of her face drooped heavy with grief. Thus she, clothed in black cloth from head to foot, as if that old past, whose child she was, stood shrouded in her form, ready to make wail for the glory of men and the beauty of women it had seen buried forever in the silent tomb.

Thus stood she for a time, as if she held
communion with the grave and death. Then
opened she her mouth, and in the mode when
song was language, she poured her feelings
forth in that old tongue, which, like some
fragrant fragment of sweet wood, borne northward by great ocean currents out of southern
seas, for many days storm tossed, but lodged
at last on some far shore and found by those
who only sense the sweetness, but know not
whence it came, lies lodged to-day upon the
mountain slopes of Spain. Thus, in the old
Basque tongue, sweet fibre of lost root, unknown to moderns, but soft, and sad, and
wild with the joy, the love, the passion of ten
thousand years, this child of the old past and
the old faiths, lifted up her voice and sang:

"O death! I hate thee! Cold thou art
and dreadful to the touch of the warm hand
and the sweet lips which, drawn by love's dear
habit, stoop to kiss the mouth for the long
parting. Cold, cold art thou, and at thy touch
the blood of men is chilled and the sweet glow
in woman's bosom frozen forever. Thou art

great nature's curse. The grape hates thee.
Its blood of fire can neither make thee laugh,
nor sing, nor dance. The sweet flower, and
the fruit which ripens on the bough, nursing
its juices from the maternal air, and the bird
singing his love-song to his mate amid the
blossoms—hate thee! At touch of thine, O
slayer! the flower fades, the fruit withers and
falls, and the bird drops dumb into the grasses.
Thou art the shadow on the sunshine of the
world; the skeleton at all feasts; the mar-
plot of great plans; the stench which fouls
all odors; the slayer of men and the murderer
of women. O death! I, child of an old race,
last leaf from a tree that shadowed the world,
warm in my youth, loving life, loving health,
loving love. O death! how I hate thee!"

Thus she sang, her full tones swelling fuller
as she sang, until her voice sent its clear
challenge bravely out to the black shadow on
the sunshine of the world and the dread fate
she hated.

Then did she a strange thing; a rite known
to the morning of the world when all the liv-

ing lived in the east and the dead went west
ward.

She took a gourd, filled to the brown brim,
and placed it in the dead man's stiffened
hand, then laid a rounded loaf beside his knee,
and on a plate of copper at his feet—serpent
edged, and in the centre a pictured island
lying low and long in the blue seas, bold with
bluff mountains toward the east, but sinking
westward until it ran from sight under the
ocean's rim, a marvel of old art in metal working, lost for aye—she placed a living coal,
and on it, from a golden acorn at her throat,
which opened at touch, she shook a dust,
which, falling on the coal, burned rosy red
and filled the hall with languous odors sweet
as Heaven. Then, at triumphant pose, she
stood and sang:

Water for thy thirst I have given,
  Hurry on ! hurry on !
Bread for thy hunger beside thee,
  Speed away ! speed away !
Fire for thy need at thy feet,
Mighty chief, fly fast and fly far   [waiting.
To the land where thy father and clansmen are

Odor and oil for the woman thou lovest,
Sweet and smooth may she be on thy breast,
 When her soft arms enfold thee.

O death! thou art cheated!
He shall thirst never more;
He shall eat and be filled;
The fire at his feet will revive him;
Oil and odor are his for the woman he loves;
He shall live, he shall live on forever
 With his sires and his people.
He shall love and be loved and be happy.

O! death grim and great,
O! death stark and cold,
By a child of the old race that first lived
 And first met thee;
The race that lived first, still lives
 And will live forever.
By a child of the old blood, by a girl!
 Thou art cheated!

CHAPTER III.

EVENING was on the woods. The girl sat reading her mother's message, taken from the golden chest that owned the golden key. And this is what she read:

"My daughter: They tell me I must die. I know it, for a chill, strange to my blood, is creeping through and thickening in my veins. It is the old tale told from the beginning of the world—of warm blood frozen when 'tis warmest, and beauty blasted at its fullest bloom. For I am at that age when woman's nature gives most and gets most from sun and flower, from touch of baby hands and man's strong love, and all the blood within her moves, tremulous with forces whose working makes her pure and sweet, as moves the strong wine

64

in the cask when ripening its red strength and flavor. O daughter of a race that never lied save for a loved one! blood of my blood, remember that your mother died hating to die; died when life was fullest, sweetest, fiercest in her; for life is passionate force, and when full is fierce to crave, to seek, to have and hold, and has been so since man loved woman and by woman was beloved. And so it is with me. A woman, I crave to live, and, craving life, must die.

"Death! how I hate thee! What right hast thou to claim me now when I am at my sweetest? The withered and the wrinkled are for thee. For thee the colorless cheek, the shriveled breast, the skinny hand that shakes as shakes the leaf, frost smitten to its fall, the lustreless eye, and the lone soul that looketh longingly ahead where wait its loved ones; such are for thee, not I. For I am fair and fresh and full through every vein of those quick forces, which belong to life, and hate the grave. This, that you may know your mother died unwillingly, and in death hated death, as all of the old race and faith have done since he first came, a power, a mystery and a curse into the world. For in the ancient annals of our fathers it was written ' that in the beginning of the world there was no death, but life was all in all.' God talked with them as father talks with children ; their daughters were married to His sons, and earth and heaven were one.

"Your father was of France, but also of that blood next oldest ours. He was Lenape, a branch blown from that primal tree which was the world's first growth, whose roots ran under ocean before the first world sank ; a branch blown far by fate, which, falling, struck deep into the soil of this western world, and, vital with deathless sap, grew and became a tree. This was in ancient days, when thoughts of men were writ in pictures and the round world rested on a Tortoise's back—emblem of water. For the first world was insular, and blue seas washed it from end to end, a mighty stretch, which reached from sunrise into sunset, through many zones. Long after men lost knowledge and the earth was flat, and for a thousand years the Tortoise symbol was an unread riddle save to us of the old blood, who knew the pictured tongue, and laughed to see the later races, mongrel in blood and rude, flatten out the globe of God until it lay flat as their ignorance. Your father was Lenape, who bore upon his breast the Tortoise symbol of old knowledge made safe by sacredness; for the wise men of his race, that the old fact might not be lost, but borne safely on like a dry seed blown over deserts until it comes to water, and, lodging, finds chance to grow into a full flowered, fruitful tree, made it, when they died and knowledge passed, the Totem of his tribe. Thus the dead symbol kept the living fact alive. Nor was there lacking other proofs that his blood was one with mine, though reaching us through world-wide channels. For in his tongue, like flecks of gold in heaps of common sand, were words of the old language, clear and bright with the original lustre, when gold was sacred ornament and had no vulgar use. The mongrel moderns have made it base and fouled it with dirty trade; but in the beginning, and by those of primal blood, who knew they were of heaven, it was a sacred metal, held for God.[18]

"We met in France, and by French custom were allied. I was a girl, and knew not my own self, and he a boy scarce twenty. Reasons of state there were to prompt our marriage, and so we were joined. He was of our old blood. That drew me, and no other thing, for love moved not within me, but nested calmly in my breast as a young bird, ere yet its wings are grown or it has thrilled with flight, rests in its downy cincture. He died at Mamelons; died under doom. You know the tale. He died and you came, fatherless, into the world.

"You are your mother's child. In face and

---

[18] Among many of the ancient races gold and silver were sacred metals, not used in commerce, but dedicated as votive offerings, or sent to the temples as dues to the gods. Nothing more astonished and puzzled the natives of Peru and Mexico than the eagerness with which the Spaniards sought for gold, and the high value they put upon it. A West Indian savage traded a handful of gold dust with one of the sailors with Columbus for some small tool, and then ran as for his life to the woods, lest the sailor should repent his bargain and demand the tool to be given back!

form, in eye and every look, you are of me and not of him. The French cross in his blood made weakness, and the stronger blood prevailed. This is the law. A turbid stream sinks with quick ebb; the pure flows level on. The Jews prove this. The ancient wisdom stands in them. The creed, which steals from their old faith, whatever makes it strong, has armed the world against them, but their blood triumphs. The old tide, red and true, unmixed, pure, laughs at these mongrel streams. Strong with pure strength it bides its time. The world will yet be theirs, and so the prophecy of their sacred books be met. Pure blood shall win, albeit muddy veins to-day are boasted of by fools.

" But we are older far than they. The Jews are children, while on our heads the rime of hoary time rests white as snow. Our race was old when Egypt, sailing from our ancestral ports, reached, as a colony, the Nile.[19] From

[19] It is certain that the Iberian race settled on the Spanish peninsula a long time before the Egyptians, a sister colony from the same unknown parental source, doubtless, began their marvelous structures on the Nile.

tideless Sea,[20] to the Green Island in the west,[21] from southern Spain to Arctic zones, the old Basque banner waved; while under Mamelons, where waits the doom for insult to pure blood, your fathers anchored ships from the beginning. What loss came to the earth when the gods of the old world, of whom we are, sank under sea and with them took the perfect knowledge! Alas! alas! the chill creeps in and on and I must hurry! I would make you wise before I die with a wisdom which none save the women of our race might speak or learn.

" You will read this when I am fixed among the women of our race in the great realms where they are queens. For since the first the women of our race have ruled and had their way, whether for good or ill, and both have come to them and through them unto others. And so forever will it be. For beauty is a fate, and unto what 'tis set none know. The issue proves it and nought else. So be

[20] The Mediterranean.
[21] Ireland.

it. She who has the glory of the fate should
have the courage to bide issue.

"Your body is my body ; your face my face ;
your blood my blood. The warmth of the
old fires are in it, and the sweet heat which
glows in you will make you understand. You
are my child, and being so, I give you of my·
self. I love. Love as the women of our race
and only they may love. Love with a love
that maketh all my life so that without it all
is death to me. That love I, dying, bestow
on you. It came to me like flash of fire
on altar when holy oils are kindled and the
censer swung. Here I first met him. Death
had me. He fought and took me from his
hand. In the beginning, men were large and
strong, and women beautiful. Giants were on
the earth, and our mothers wedded them.
Each was a rose, thorn-guarded, and the
strongest plucked her when in bloom and
wore her, full of sweets, upon his bosom.
Since then the women of our blood have loved
large men. Weak ones we hated. None save
the mighty, brawny, and brave have ever felt

our soft arms round them, or our mouths on theirs. Thus has it been.

"I loved him, for his strength was as the ancients, and with it gentleness like the gods. But he was humble, and knew not his own greatness, and, blinded by humility, he would not see that I was his. So I waited, waited as all women wait, that they may win. It is not art, but nature, the nature of a rose, which, daily opening more and more to perfect bloom in his warm light, makes the sun know his power at last. For love reveals all greatness in us, as it does all faults. Well did I know that he should see at last his fitness for me, and, without violence to himself, yield to my loveliness and be drawn within the circle of my arms. So should I win at last, as have the women of our race won always. But death mars all. So has it been since women lived. His is the only knife whose edge may cut the silken bonds we wind round men. Vain is all else. Faiths may not stand against us, nor pride, nor honor. Our power draws stronger. The grave alone makes gap 'twixt lovely woman's loving and bridal bed. So, dying thus before my time I am bereft of all.

"But you shall win, for in you I shall live again and to full time. I know that you will love him, for you drew my passion to you with my milk, and all my thoughts were of him, when, with large, receptive eyes, you lay a baby in my arms, day after day, scanning my face, love-lighted for him. Aye, you will love him. For in your sleep, cradled on the heart that worshiped him, its warmth for him warmed you, its beating thrilled, and from my mouth, murmured caressingly in dreams, your ears and tongue learned his dear name before mine own. So art thou fated unto love as I to death. Both could not win, and hence, perhaps, 'tis well I die. For had both lived, then both had loved, mother and child been rivals, and one suffered worse than dying. Nor am I without joy. For once, when I was wooing him with art he did not know, coaxing him up to me with sweet praises sweetly said, and purposely I swayed so my warm body fell into his arms and there lay for a

moment, vibrant, all aglow, while all my
woman's soul went through my lifted and
dimmed eyes to him, I saw a flash of fire
flame in his face, and felt a throb jump
through his body, as the God woke in him,
which told me he was mortal. And, faint
with joy, I slid downward from his arms and
in the fragrant grasses sat, throbbing, covering up my face with happy hands lest he
should see the glory of it and be frightened
at what his touch had done. I swear by the
old blood, that moment's triumph honored,
that the memory of that blissful time takes
the sting from death and robs the grave of
victory, as I lie dying.

"Yea, thou shalt win. The power will be in
thee, as it has been in me, to win him or any
whom women made as we set heart on. But
woo him with that old art of innocence, snow
white, though hot as fire, lost to the weak or
brazen women of these mongrel races that fill
the world to-day, who dare not dare, or daring,
overdo. Be slow as sunrise. Let thy love
dawn on him as morning dawns upon the

earth, and warmth and light grow evenly, lest
the quick flash blind him, or the sudden
heat appall, and he see nothing right, but
shrink from thee and his new self as from a
wicked thing. I may not help thee. What
fools these moderns are to think so. The
dead have their own lives and loves, and note
not the living. Else none might be at peace
or know comfort above the sky, and all souls
would make wail for wrongs and woes done
and borne under sun. So is it well that parting should be parting, and what wall divides
the dead from living be beyond penetra-
tion. For each woman's life is sole. Her
plans are hidden with her love. Her skill is
of it a sweet secrecy, and all her winning is
self-won. I do not fear. Thou wilt have the
wooing wisdom of thy race. Thy eyes are
such as men give life to look into. The passion in thy blood would purchase thrones.
Thou hast the grace of form which maddens
men. Thy voice is music. Thy touch warm
velvet to the skin. The first and perfect
woman lives complete, in thee!

" No more. In the old land no one is left. The modern cancer eats all there. New fashions and new faiths crowd in. Only low blood is left, and that soon yields to pelf and pain. Last am I of the queenly line and thou art last of me. I came of gods. I go to gods. The tree that bore the fruit of knowledge for our sex in the sunrise of the world is stripped to the last sweet leaf. If thou shalt die leaving no root, the race God made is ended. With thee the gods quit earth, and the old red blood beats back and upward to the skies. Gold hast thou and broad acres. Youth and health are thine. Win his great strength to thee, for he is pure as strong, and from a primal man get perfect children, that in this new world in the west a new race may arise rich in old blood, born among the hills, strong with the strength of trees, whose sons shall be as mountains, and whose daughters as the lakes, whose loveliness is lovelier because of the reflected mountains dimly seen in them.

"Farewell. Love greatly. It is the only way that leadeth woman to her heaven. The moderns have a saying in their creed that God is love. In the beginning he was Father. The race that sprung from Him said that, and said no more. It was enough. Love then was human, and we gloried in it. Not the pale love of barren nun, but love red as the rose, warm as the sun, the love of motherly women, sweet mouthed, deep breasted, voiced with cradle songs and soft melodies which made men love their homes. Love thou and live on the old level. Be not ashamed to be full woman. Love strength. Bear children to it. Be mother of a mighty race born for this western world. Multiply. Inherit; and send the old blood flowing from thy veins, a widening current, thrilling through the ages; that it may be as red, as pure, as strong at sunset as it was in the sunrise of the world.

"Once more, farewell, sweet daughter. These are last words, a voice from out the sunset, sweet and low as altar hymn wandering down the columned aisles of some old temple. So may it sound to thee. So live, so woo, so win, that when thou comest through the por-

tals of the west to that fair throne amid
those other ones which stretch their state-
liness across the endless plain of ended
things, which waits for thee as one has
waited for every woman of our queenly line,
thou shalt leave behind at going a new and
noble race, from thee and him, in which the
east and west, the sunrise and the sunset of
the world shall, like two equal glories, meet
condensed and shine. So fare thee well. Fear
not Mamelons. For if thou failest there, thou
shalt be free of fault, and all the myriad millions of our blood shall out of sunset march,
and from the shining sands of fate lift thee
high and place thee on the last, the highest,
and the whitest throne of our old line. So
ends it. One more sweet kiss, sweet one. One
more long look into his face—grave, grave and
sad he gazeth at me. God! What a face he
has! Shall I find match for it to-morrow when
I stand, amid the royal, beyond sunset? Perhaps. Death, you have good breeding. You
have waited well. Come, now, I will go on
with thee. Yes, yes, I see the way. 'Tis very

plain. It has been hollowed by so many feet. Good-bye to earthly light and life. It may be I shall find a better. I'll know to-morrow."

Here the scroll ended. Long the living sat pondering what the dead had writ. She kissed the writing as it were holy text. Then placed it in the chest, and turned the golden key and said: " Sweet mother, thou shalt live in me. Our race shall not die out. My love shall win him." Then went she to the great room where the trapper sat by the red fire and said: " John Norton, thou art my guest. What may I do to pleasure thee? Here thou must stay until my mind can order out my life and make the dubious road ahead look plain. While underneath my roof, I pray, command me."

All this with such grave dignity and sweet grace as she were queen and he some kinsman, great and wise.

The trapper stooped and lifted a huge log upon the fire, which broke the lower brands. The chimney roared, and the large room brightened to the flame. Then, facing her, he said:

"Guest I am and servant, both in one, and must be so awhile. Winter is on us. The fire feels snow. It putters as if the flakes were falling in it. It is a sign that never lies. Hark! you can hear the konk of geese as they wedge southward. The winter will be long, but I must stay."

"And are you sorry you must stay?" replied the girl. "I will do what I may to make the days and nights pass swiftly."

"Nay, nay, you do mistake," returned the trapper. "I am not sorry for myself, but thee. If I may only help thee: how can I help thee?"

"John Norton," replied the girl, and she spoke with sweet earnestness as when the heart is vocal, "thou art a man, and wise; I am a girl, and know naught save books. But you, you have seen many men and tribes of men; counciled with chiefs, been comrade with the great, sharing their inner thoughts in peace and war, and thou hast done great deeds thyself, of which fame speaks widely. Why do you cheapen your own value so, calling thyself a common man? My uncle said you were the best, the bravest, and the wisest man he ever met, and he had sat with kings and chiefs, and heard the best men of both worlds tell all they knew. Dear friend, wilt thou not be my teacher, and teach me many things, which lieth now, like treasures hidden, locked in thy silence ?"

"I teach thee!" exclaimed the trapper. "I, an unlettered man, a hunter of the woods, teach one who readeth every tongue, who knoweth all the past, to the beginning of the world, whose head has in it all these shelves of knowledge," and the trapper swept a gesture toward the long rows of books that thickened one side of the great hall from floor to ceiling. "I teach thee!"

"Yes, you," answered the girl. "You can teach me, or any woman that ever lived, or any man. For you were given at your birth the seeing eye, the listening ear, and the still patience of the mountain cat, which on the bare bough sits watching, from sunset until sunrise, motionless. In the old days such gifts meant wisdom, wider, deeper, more exact

than that of books, for so my mother often
told me. She said the wisest men who ever
lived were those who, in deep woods and caves
and on the shore of seas, saw, heard, and
pondered on the life and mysteries of nature,
noting all things, small and great, cause and
effect, tracing out connections which interlace
the parts into one whole, so making one solid
woof of knowledge, covering all the world of
fact and substance in the end. And once,
when you were in the mood, and had been
talking in the hall, drawn on and out by her,
you told of climes and places you had seen,
and strange things met in wandering, of great
mounds builded by some ancient race, long
dead; of cities, under sunset, still standing
solid, without men; of tall and shapely pil-
lars, writ with mystic characters, on the far
shore of the mild sea, whence sailed the old
dead of my race, at dying, far away to western
heavens, where to-day they live; of caverns in
deep earth, made glorious with crystals, sta-
lactites, prisms, and shining ornaments, where,
in old time, the gods of the under world were

chambered; of trees that mingled bloom and
fruitage the long year through, and flowers
that never faded till the root died out; of
creeping reptiles, snakes, and savage poison-
ous things that struck to kill, and of their
antidotes, growing for man and beast amid the
very grasses where they secreted venom; of
rivers wide and deep, boiling up through solid
earth, full-tided, which, flowing widely on,
dropped suddenly like a plummet to the centre of the world; of plains, fenced by the sky,
far reaching as the level sea, so that the red
sun rose and set in grasses; of fires, which lit
by lightning, blackened the stars with smoke
and burned all the world; of oceans in the
west, which, flowing with joint floods, fell over
mountains, plunging their weights of water
sheer downward, so that their rocky framework of the round earth shook; of winds that
blew as out of chaos, revolving on a hollow
axis like a wheel buzzing, invisible, charged
to the centre with electric force, and fires
which burst explosive, kindling the air like
tinder; and of ten thousand marvels and curi-

ous things, which you had met, noted, and pondered on, seeking to know the primal fact or force which underlaid them. So that my mother said that night, when we were in our chamber, that you were the wisest man she ever met; wise with the wisdom of her ancient folk, whose knowledge lived, oral and terse, before the habit of bookmaking came to rive the solid substance, heavy and rich, into thin veneer, to make vain show for fools to wonder at. Teach me! Who might thou not teach, thou seeing, silent man, type of my first fathers, who, gifted with rare senses and with wit to question nature and to learn, mastered all wisdom before books were."

"Aye, aye," returned the trapper, not displeased to hear her praise as rare what seemed to him so common, "these things I know in truth, for I have wandered far, seen much, and noted closely, and he who sleeps in woods has time to think. But, girl, I am an unlearned man, and know naught of books."

"Books!" exclaimed the girl. "What are books but oral knowledge spread out in words which lack the fire of forceful utterance? But you shall know them. The winter days are short, the nights are long; our toil is simple; wood for the fire, food for the table, and a swift push each day along the snow for exercise; or, if the winds will keep some acres clean, our skates shall ring to the smitten ice, piercing it with tremblings till all the shores cry out. All other hours for sleep and books. I read in seven tongues, one so old that none save I in all the world can read it; for it was writ when letters were a mystery, known only unto those who fed the sacred fire and kept God's altars warm. And I will read you all the wisdom of the world, and its rare laughter, which, mother said, was the fine effervesce of wisdom, the pungent foam and sparkle of it. So you shall know. And one old scroll there is, rolled in foil of gold, sealed with the serpent seal, symbol of eternity, scribed with pictured knowledge, an heirloom of my race, whose key alone I have, writ in rainbow colors, when the world was young, the language of the gods, who first made signs for speech and

put the speaking mouth upon a page. It was
the first I learned. My mother taught it to
me standing at her knee—for so the law says
it shall be done, a law old with twice ten
thousand years of age—that he who knows
this scroll shall teach it, under silence, to his
or her first born, standing at knee, that the
old knowledge of prime things and days may
not perish from the earth it tells of, but live
on forever while the earth endures. For on it
is the record of the beginning, told by those
who saw it; of the first man and how he came
to be; of woman, first, when born and of what
style. A list of healing simples, antidotes
'gainst death, and of rare oils which search
the bones and members of the mortal frame
and banish pain ; and others yet, sweet to the
nose, and volatile, that make the face to shine,
for feasts and happy days, and being poured
on women, make their skin softer than down,
whiter than drifted snow, and so clean and
clear that the rich blood pinks through it like
a red rose centred in crystal. And on it, too,
is written other and strange rules, wild and

weird. How one may have the seeing eye
come to him. How to call up the wicked
dead from under ground, and summon from
their heaven in the west, where they live and
love, the blessed. How marriage came to man
with woman. What part is his to act and
what part hers, that each may be a joy to
other, and she, thus honored, be as sweet slip
grafted on a vital trunk, full flowered in fullest
growth, and fruitful of what the old gods
loved, children, healthy, fair, and strong; all
will I read thee, talking as we read, that we,
with sharpened thought, may bite through to
the vital gist, deep centred within the hard
rind of words, and taste the living sweetness
of true sense. So will we teach each other
and grow wise equally; you, me the knowledge of things and places you have seen, I,
you the knowledge writ in books that I have
read."

CHAPTER IV.

LOVE'S VICTORY.

NEXT day, the trapper's sign proved true. Winter fell whitely on the world. Its soft fleece floated downward to the earth whiter than washed wools. The waters of the lake blackened in contrast to the shores. The flying leaves—tardy vagrants from the branch—were smothered mid the flakes, and dropped like shot birds. Toward night the wind arose. The forest moaned heavily. At sunset, in the gray gloom, a flock of ducks soared southward through the whirling storm. A field of geese, leaderless, bewildered, blinded by the driving flakes, scented water, and, like a noisy mob, fell, with a mighty splash, into the lake. Summer went with the day, and with the night came winter, white,

88

cold, and stormy, roaring violently through the air.

In the great hall sat the two. The logs, piled on the wide hearth, glowed red—a solid coal from end to end, cracked with concentric rings. They reddened the hall, books, skins, and antlered trophies of the chase. The strong man and the girl's dark face stood forth in the warm luminance, pre-Raphaelite. The trapper sat in a great chair, built solidly of rounded wood, untouched by tool, but softly cushioned. The girl, recumbent, rested on a pile of skins, black with the glossy blackness of the bear, full furred. Her dress, a garnet velvet, from the looms of France. Her moccasins, snow white. On either wrist a serpent coil of gold. A diamond at her throat. A red fez on her head, while over her rich dress the glossy masses of her hair fell tangled to her feet. She read from an old book, bound with rich plush, whose leaves were vellum, edged with artful garniture and lettered richly with crimson ink—a precious relic of old literature, saved from those vandal flames which burned

the stored knowledge of the world to ashes at
Alexandria. The characters were Phœnician,
and told the story of that race to which we
owe our modern alphabet; whose ships, a thousand years before the Christ, went freighted
with letters, seeking baser commerce, to every
shore of the wide world. She read by the red
firelight, and the ruddy glow fell vividly on
the pictured page, the rich dress outlining her
full form and the swarth beauty of her face.
It was the story of an old race—no library has
it now—the story of their rise, their glory, and
their fall. She read for hours, pausing here
and there to tell her listener of connecting
things—of Rome that was not then ; of Greece
yet to be born ; of Egypt, swarming on the
Nile and building monuments for eternity,
and of her ancient race, west of the tideless sea,
whose annals, even then, reached backward
through ten thousand years, thus making clear
what otherwise were dark, and teaching him
all history. So passed the hours till midnight
struck. Then she arose, and lifting goblet
half-filled with water, poured it on the hearth,

saying: " I spill this water to a race whose going emptied half the world." This solemnly, for she was of the past, and held to its old fashions, knowing all its symbolism, its rites, its daily customs, and what they meant, for so she had been taught, and nothing else, by her whose blood and beauty she repeated. Then she took the trapper's hand and laid it on her head, bent low, and said : " Dear friend, I am so glad to serve you. I have enjoyed this night beyond all nights I ever knew. I hope for many others like to it, and even sweeter." And saying this she looked with glad and peaceful eyes into his face, and glided noiselessly from the room.

The trapper piled high the logs again, and, lying down upon the skins where she had lain, gazed with wide eyes into the coals. The gray was in the sky before he slept, and in his sleep he murmured: "It cannot be. I am an unlearned man and poor. I am not fit." Above him in her chamber, nestling in sleep, the girl sighed in her dreams and murmured: " How blind he is !" And then: " My love shall win him !"

Dear girl, sweet soul of womanhood, gift to these gilded days from the old solid past, I would the thought had never come to me to tell this tale of Mamelons!

So went the winter; and so the two grew upward side by side in knowledge. He learning of the past as taught in books; of men long dead whose names had been unknown to him; of deeds done by the mighty of the world; of cities, monuments, tombs long buried; of races who mastered the world and died mastered by their own weakness; of faiths, philosophies, and creeds once bright and strong as fire, now cold and weak as sodden ashes; of vanished rites and mysteries and lost arts which once were the world's wonder—all were unfolded to him, so that his strong mind grasped the main point of each and understood the whole. And she learned much from him; of bird and beast and fish; of climates and their growths; of rocks and trees; of nature's signs and movements by day and night; of wandering tribes and mongrel races; the lore of woods and waters and the differences in governments which shape the lives of men. So taught they each the other; she, swift of thought and full of eastern fire; he, slower minded, but calm, sagacious, comprehensive, remembering all and settling all in wise conclusion. Two better halves, in mind and soul and body, to make a perfect whole, were never brought by fate together since God made male and female. The past and present, fire and wood, fancy and judgment, beauty to win and strength to hold, sound minds in sound bodies, the perfect womanhood and manhood ideal, typical, met, conjoined in them.

Slowly she won him. Slowly she drew him, with the innocence of loving, to oneness in wish and thought and feeling, with her sweet self. Slowly, as the moon lifts the great tide, she lifted him toward her, until his nature stood highest, full flooded, nigh, bathed in all the wide, deep flowing of its greatness, in her white radiance. It was an angel's mission, and all the wild passion of her blood, barbaric, original, was sobered with reverent thought of the great destiny that she, wedded to him, stood heir to. She had no other hope, nor wish, nor dream, than to be his. She was all woman. This life was all to her. She had no future. If she had, she wisely put it by until she came to it. She took no thought of far to-morrow. Sufficient for the day was the joy or sorrow of it. She lived. She loved. That was enough. What more might be to woman than to live, to love, worship her husband and bear children? Such life were heaven. If other heaven there was she could not crave it, being satisfied. So felt she. So had she felt. So acted that it might be; and now, at last, she stood on that white line each perfect woman climbs to, passing which, radiant, content, grateful, she enters heaven.

   *   *   *   *   *   *   *   *

Spring came. Heat touched the snow, and it grew liquid. The hills murmured as with many tongues, and low music flowed rippling down their sides. The warm earth sweetened with odors. Sap stirred in root and bough, and the fibred sod thrilled with delicious passages of new life.

From the far South came flaming plumage, breasts of gold and winged music to the groves. The pent roots of herbs, spiced and pungent, burst upward through the moistened mould, and breathed wild, gamy odors through the woods. The skeleton trees thickened with leaf formations, and hid their naked grayness under green and gold. Each day birds of passage, pressed by parental instinct, slanted wings toward the lake, and, sailing inward, to secluded bays, made haste to search for nests. Mother otters swam heavy through the tide, and the great turtles, lumbering from the water, digged deep pits under starlight, in the sand, and cunningly piled their pyramid of eggs. All nature loved and mated, each class of life in its own order, and God began the recreation of the world.

The two were standing under leafy screen on the lake's shore, the warm sun overhead and the wide water lying level at their feet. Nature's mood was on them, and their hearts, like equal atmospheres, flowed to sweet union. Reverently they spoke, as soul to soul, con-

cealing nothing, having nothing to conceal, of
their deep feeling and of duty unto each.
The girl held up her clean, sweet nature unto
him, that he might see it, wholly his forever;
and he kept nothing back. She knew he
loved her, and to her the task to make him
feel the honor she received in being loved by
him. So stood they, alone in the deep woods,
apart from men, in grave, sweet counsel.
Thus spake the man :

"I love you, Atla; you know it. I would
lay down my life for you. But our marriage
may not be. I am too old."

"Too old!" replied the girl. "Thou hast
seen forty years, I twenty. Thou art the riper,
sweeter, better; that is all. I would not wed
a boy. The women of our race have wedded
men, big bodied, strong to fight, to save, to
make home safe, their country free, and fame,
that richest heritage to children. My mother
broke the rule, and rued it. She might have
rued it worse had death not cut the tighten-
ing error which knotted her to coming torture.
My heart holds hard to the old law made for

the women of our race by ancient wisdom;
'Wed not boys, but wed grave and gentle men.
For women would be ruled, and who, of pride
and fire, would be ruled by striplings.' And
again: 'Let ivy seek the full-grown oak, nor
cling to saplings.' I love the laws that were,
love the old faiths and customs. They filled
the world with beauty and brave men. They
gave great nature opportunity to keep great,
kept noble blood from base, strength from
wedding weakness, and barred out mongrel-
ism from the world, which in the ancient days
was deadliest sin, corrupting all. O love! you
do mistake, saying 'I am too old.' For
women have ever the child's habit in them.
They love to be held in arms, love to look up
to loving eyes, love to be commanded, and
obey strong sovereignty. The husband is
head—head of the house. He sits in wide
authority, and from his wisdom flow counsel,
command, which all the house, wife, children,
and servants, bend to, obedient. How can a
stripling fill such seat? How sit such dignity on a beardless face? How, save from

seasoned strength, such safety come to all? O full grown man! be oak to me, and let me twine my weakness round thy strength, that I may find safe lodgment, nor be shaken in my roots when storms blow strong. Too old! I would thy head were sown with the white rime of added years. So should I love thee more!"

Ah me, such pleading from love's mouth, such sweet entreaty from love's heart man never heard before, in these raw days, when callow youth is fondled by weak women, and boys with starting beards push wisdom, gray and grave, from council chairs.

"Atla, it cannot be. I will admit that you say, sooth, my years do not forbid. Boys are rash, hot-headed, quick of tongue, ill-mannered, lacking patience, just sense, and slow-mannered gentleness which comes with added years, and that deep knowledge which slows blood and gentles speech, and I do see that you fit well to these, and would be happier with a man thus charactered. But, letting that go by—and all my heart is grateful that

it may—still marriage may not be between us,
for thou art rich and I am poor, and so it
should not be. For husband should own
house; the wife make home. What say you,
am I right or wrong?"

To which the girl made answer: "Thou
art an old-time man, John Norton, and this
judgment fits the ancient wisdom. For in the
beginning so it was. The male built nest, the
female feathered it with song. So each had
part in common ministry. The man was
greater, richer, than the woman, and with
earthly substance did endow. And she in turn
gave sweet companionship, and sang loneliness from his life with mother songs and children's prattle. Thus in the beginning. Yea,
thou art right, as thou art always right. For,
being sound in heart and head, thou canst not
err. Thy judgment goes straight to the centre of the truth as goes thy bullet. But as
men lived and died change came to the first
order. For men without male issue died and
left great dower to girls. Women, by no fault
of theirs, nor lack of modesty, grew rich by

gifts of death, which are the gifts of fate. And
changing circumstance changed all, making
the old law void. The gods pondered, and a
new order rose. By chance, at first, then by
ordainment, royalty left male and followed female blood, because their blood was truer to
itself, less vagrant, purer, better kept. And
women of red blood and pure, clothed in royalty from shame, made alliances with men
whom their souls loved, and gave rank, wealth,
and their sweet selves in lavishness of loving,
which gives all and keeps nothing back. Such
was the habit of my race and line from age to
age, even as I read you from the pictured scroll,
rolled in foil of gold, that only I, of all the
world, can read; and if I die, leaving no child,
the golden secret goes with me to the gods,
and all the ancient lore is lost to men forever.
This to assist your judgment and make the
scales hang level from your hand for just de-
cision. Am I to blame because I stand as heir
to ancient blood and wealth? Shall these wide
acres, gold in yonder house, gems in casket,
and diamonds worn for ten thousand years by

women of my race, queens of the olden time,
when in their hands they lifted world-wide
sceptres, divide thee and me? Has love no
weight in the just scales you, by the working
of some old fate, I know not what, hold over
me and my soul's wish to-day? Be just to
your own soul, be just to mine, and fling these
doubts aside as settled forever by the mighty
Power that works in darkness, and through
darkness, to the light, shaping our fates and
ordering life and death, joy and grief, beyond
our power to fix or change. Blown by two
winds, whose coming and going we list not,
we, two, meet here. Strong art thou and weak
am I, but shall thy strength repel my weakness? Rich, without fault, I am. My blood
is older than these hills, purer than yonder
water, and wilt thou make an accident, light
as a feather in just balances, outweigh a fact
sweet as heaven, heavy as fate? The queens
of old, whose blood is one with mine, who
spake the self-same tongue and loved the self-
same way, chose men to be their kings; so I,
by the same law, choose thee. Be thou my

king.   Rule me in love.   By the old right and
rule of all my race, I place thy hand upon my
head, and so pass under yoke.   I am thy subject, and all my days shall be a sweet subjection.   Do with me as thou wilt.   I make no
terms.   My feet shall walk with thine to the
dark edge of death. Farther I know not. This
life we may make sure.   The next is or is not
ours to order.   No man may say.   Lord of my
earthly life, take me, take me to thy arms, that
I, last of an old race, last of its blood, left sole
in all the world, without father, mother, friend,
may feel I am beloved by him I worship, and
drink one glad, sweet cup before I go to touch
the bitter edge of dubious chance at Mamelons."

Then love prevailed.   Doubt went from out
his soul.   His nature, unrestrained, leaped up
in a red rush of joy to eyes and face.   He
lifted hands and opened arms to her.   To
them she swept, as bird into safe thicket,
chased by hawk, with a glad cry.   Panting
she lay upon his bosom, trembling through all
her frame, placed mouth to his and lost all
sense but feeling.   Then, with a gasp, drew

back and lifted dewy eyes to his, as fed child lifts hers to nursing mother's face, or saint her worshiping gaze to God.

But the gods of her old race, standing beyond sunset, lifted high, saw, farther on, the sandy slope of Mamelons, and, while she lay in heaven on her lover's breast, they bent low their heads and wept.

*   *   *   *   *   *   *   *

Spring multiplied its days and growths. Night followed night as star follows star in their far circuits, wheeling forever on. Each morn brought sweet surprise to each. For like the growths of nature so grew their love fuller with bloom each morn; with fragrance fuller each dewy night. Her nature, under love's warmth, grew richer, seeding at its core for sweeter, larger life. His borrowed tone and color from her own, and fragrance. So, in the happy days of the long spring, as earth grew warmer, sweeter with the days, the two grew, with common growth and closer, until they stood in primal unity, no longer twain, but one.

One day she came to him, and put her hand in his and said :

" Dear love, there is an old rite by which my people married. It bindeth to the grave; no farther. For there the old faith stopped, not knowing what life might be beyond, or by whom ordered. Thine goeth on through death as light through darkness, and holds the hope that earthly union lasts forever. It may be so. Perhaps the Galilean knew better than the gods what is within the veil, for so the symbol is. It is a winning faith. My heart accepts it as a happy chance; and, did it not, it would not matter. Thy faith is mine, and thine shall be my God. Perchance the ancient deities and your modern One are but the same, with different names. We worshiped ours with fruits and flowers and incense; with dancing feet, glad songs, and altars garlanded with flowers; moistened with wine; you, yours with doleful music, bare rites, the beggary of petition and cold reasoning. Our fashion was the better, for it kept the happy habits up of children, gladly grateful for father gifts, and so pro-

longed the joyous childhood of the world.
But in this thy faith is better—it hangs a star
above the tide of death for love to steer by.
My heart accepts the sign. Thy faith is mine.
We will go down to Mamelons, and there be
married by the holy man who wears upon his
breast the sign you trust to."

"Nay, nay; it shall not be," exclaimed the
trapper. "Atla, thou shalt not go to Mamelons. There waits the doom for the mixed
blood. There died thy father, and all its sands
are full of moldering men. We will be married here by the old custom of thy people, and
God, who looketh at the heart and knoweth all,
will bless us."

"Dear love," returned the girl, "thy word is
law to me. I have no other. It shall be as
thou wilt. But listen to my folly or my wisdom, I know not which it is: I fear not Mamelons. There is no coward blood in me. The
women of our race face fate with open eyes.
So it has been from the beginning. Death
sees no pallor in our cheeks. To love we say
farewell, then graveward go with steady steps.

The women of my house—a lengthy line, stretching downward from the past beyond annals—whose blood flows red in me, lived queens, and, dying, died as they lived. I would die so ; lest, if thy faith is true, they would not own me kin nor give me place among them when I came, if I feared fate or death. Besides, the doom may not hold good toward me. I know my uncle saw the sight ; but he was only Tortoise, a branch blown far from the old tree and lost a thousand years amid strange peoples, and his sight, therefore, could not be sure. Moreover, love, if the curse holds, and I am under doom, how may I escape ? For fate is fate, and he who runs, runs quickest into it. So let us go, I pray, to Mamelons, and there be married by the holy man, the symbol[22] on whose breast was known to our old race and carved on altars ten thousand years before the

---

[22] The cross as a symbol is traceable through all the old races, even the remotest in point of time. It was originally a symbol of plenty and joy, and so stood emblematic of happiness for tens of thousands of years. The Romans connected it with their criminal law, as we have the gallows, and so it became a symbol of shame and sorrow.

simple Jew was born at Bethlehem. So shall
the symbol of the old faith and the new be for
the first time kissed by two who represent the
sunrise and the sunset of the world; and the
god of morning and of evening be proved to be
the same, though worshiped under different
names."

He yielded, and the two made ready to set
face toward Mamelons.

There was, serving in her house, an old red
servitor, who had been chief, in other days, of
Mistassinni.[23] His dwindled tribe lives still

[23] This lake lies to the northwest of Lake St. John some 300
miles, and within some 200 miles of James' Bay. It was first
discovered by white men in the person of Pere Abanel, in 1661,
a Jesuit missionary, en route to Hudson's Bay. This is the
lake about which so much has been said in Canada and the
States, and so much printed. In fact, very little is accu-
rately known of it, unless we assume that the late survey by
Mr. Low is to be regarded as a settlement of the matter—
which few, if any, acquainted with the Mistassinni question would do. Having examined all the data bearing on
the subject, I can but conclude that the bit of water
which Mr. Low said he surveyed was only a small arm or
branch of the lake reaching south from it, and that the
Great Mistassinni itself was never seen by Mr. Low, much
less surveyed. Unless we concluded with an ancient cynic
that "All men are liars," then there surely is a vast body
of water known to the natives as Big Mistassinni, lying in
the wilderness several hundreds of miles from Hudson's

upon the lake which reaches northward beyond
knowledge. But he, longer than her life, had
lived in the great house, a life-long guest, but
serving it in his wild fashion. Warring with
Nasquapees and Mountaineers against the
Esquimaux, he had been overcome in ambush
and in the centre of their camp put to the torture. Grimly he stood the test of fire, not
making moan as their knives seamed him and
the heated spear points seared. Maddened,
one pried his jaws apart with edge of
hatchet, and tore his tongue out, saying, in
devilish jest, " If you will not talk, you have
no need of this," and ate it before his eyes.
Then the chief, with twice a hundred braves,
burst in upon them, and whirled the hellish
brood, in roaring battle, out of the world. The
trapper, plunging through whirring hatchets
and red spear points, sent the cursed fagots
flying that blazed upward to his bloody mouth

Bay, yet to be visited and surveyed by white men. Mista,
in Indian dialect, means great, and sinni means a stone or
rock. And hence Mistassinni means the " Lake of Great
Stones or Rocks." The Assinniboine, or Rocky River, Indians of the West were evidently of the same blood and language originally with these red man of the northern wilds.

and so saved him to the world. Crippled beyond hope of fighting more, he left his tribe,
and, toiling slowly through the woods, came to
the chief in the great house and said, in the
quick language of silent signs: "I am no
longer chief—I cannot fight. Let me stay here
until I die." Thus came he, and so stayed,
keeping, through many years, the larder full
of game and fish. This wrinkled, withered
man went with them, paddling his birch slowly
on, deep ladened with needed stuffs and precious things for dress and ornament at the marriage. For she said: "I will put on the
raiment of my race when my foremothers
reigned o'er half the world, and their banners,
woven of cloth of gold, dark, with an em-
erald island at the centre, waved over ships
which bore the trident at their bows, their sailors anchored under Mamelons a thousand and
a thousand years before Spain sprang a mushroom from the old Iberian mold. I will stand or
fall forever, Queen at Mamelons." So said she,
and so meant. For all her blood thrilled with
the haughty courage of that past, when fate

was faced with open, steady eyes, and the god Death, that moderns tremble at, was met by men who gazed into his gloomy orbs with haughty stare as he came blackening on. So silently the silent man went on in his light bark, loaded with robes, heavy, with flowered gold, woven of old in looms whose soft movements, going deftly to and fro, sound no more, leaving no ripple as it went, steered by his withered hands, down the black rivers of the north, toward feast or funeral under Mamelons.

CHAPTER V.

AT MAMELONS.

SUMMER was at its hottest. The woods, sweltering under heavy heat, sweat odors from every gummy pore. Flowers, unless water-rooted, withered on their stalks. The lumbering moose came to the streams and stayed. The hot hills drove him down. The feathered mothers of the streams led down their downy progeny to wider waters. The days were hot as ovens and the nights dewless. The soft sky hardened and shone brazen from pole to pole. The poplar leaves shrank from their trembling twigs and the birches shriveled in the heat. But on the rivers the air was moist and cool, lily-sweetened, and above their heads, at night, the yellow stars swung in their courses like golden globes, large, soft, and round. So the two boats went on through lovely lakes, floating slowly down the flowing rivers without hap or hazard, till they came to the last portage, beyond which flowed the Stygian[24] river, whose gloomy tide flows out of death into bright life at Mamelons.

They took the shortest trail. Straight up it ran over the mighty ridge which slopes downward, on the far side, eastward to that strange bay men call Eternity. It was an old trail only ran by runners who ran for life and death when war blazed suddenly and tribes were summoned in hot haste to rally. But she was happy hearted, and, half jesting, half in earnest, said: "Take the short trail. My heart is like a bird flying long kept from home. Let me go straight." So on the trail the two men toiled all day, while she played with the sands upon the shore and crowned herself with lilies, saying: "The queens of my old line loved lilies. I will have lily at my throat when I am wed."

[24] The waters of the Saguenay are unlike those of any other river known. They are a purple-brown, and, looked at en masse, are, to the eye, almost black. This peculiar color gives it a most gloomy and grewsome look, and serves to vastly deepen the profound impression its other peculiar characteristics make upon the mind.

Thus, when night came, the boats and all
their laden, were on the other side, and they
were on the ridge, which sloped either way,
the sunset at their backs, the gloomy gorge
ahead. Then, pausing on the crest, swept to
its rocks by rasping winds, the sunset at her
back, the gloom before, she said : " Here we
will bivouac. The sky is dewless, and the air
is cool. The trail from this runs easy down.
I would start with sunrise on my face toward
Mamelons."

So was it done, and they made camp beneath
the trees, a short walk from the ridge, where
the great spruce stood thickly, and a spring
boiled upward through the gravel, cold as ice.

The evening passed like a sweet song
through dewy air. She was so full of health,
so richly gifted, so happy in her heart, so nigh
to wedded life with him she worshiped, that
her soul was full of joyousness, as the lark's
throat, soaring skyward, is of song. She chat-
tered like a magpie in many tongues, trans-
lating rare old bits of foreign wit and ancient
mirth with apt and laughable grimaces. Her

face was mobile, rounding with jollity or lengthening with woe at will. She had the light foot and the pliant limb, the superb pose, abandon, and the languishing repose of her old race, whose princesses, with velvet feet, tinkling ankles, and forms voluptuous, lithe as snakes, danced before kings and won kingdoms with applause from those whom, by their wheeling, swaying, flashing beauty, they made wild. She danced the dances of the East, when dancing was a language and a worship, with pantomime so rare and eloquent that the pleased eye translated every motion, as the ear catches the quick speech. Then sang she the old songs of buried days, sad, wild, and sweet as love singing at death's door to memory and to hope; the song of joys departed and of joys to come. So passed the evening till the eastern stars, wheeling upward, stood in the zenith. Then with lingering lips she kissed her lover on the mouth, and on her couch of fragrant boughs fell fast asleep, forgetful of all things but life and love; murmuring softly in her happy dreams, "To-

morrow night," and after a little space, again,
" Sweet, sweet to-morrow !"

But all the long evening through, the old
tongueless chief of measureless Mistassinni
sat as an Indian sits when death is coming—
back straightened, face motionless, and eyes
fixed on vacancy. Not till the girl lay sleeping on the boughs did he stir muscle. Then
he rose up, and with dilating nostrils tested
the air, and his throat rattled. Then put his
ear to earth, as man to wall, listening to the
voices running through the framework of the
world,[25] cast cones upon the dying brands,
and, standing in the light made by the gummy
rolls, said to the trapper in dumb show : " The
dead are moving. The earth cracks beneath
the leaves. The old trail is filled with warriors hurrying eastward out of death. Their

[25] I have been often surprised at the many and strange
sounds which may at times be heard by putting my ear flat
to the sod or to the bark of trees. Even the sides of rocks
are not dumb, but often resonant with noises—of running
waters, probably—deep within. It would seem that every
formation of matter had, in some degree, the characteristics of a whispering gallery, and that, were our ears only
acute enough, we might hear all sounds moving in the
world.

spears are slanted as when men fly. They wave us downward toward the river. Call her you love from dreamland and let us go."

To which the trapper, answering, signed:

"Chief, old age is on you, and the memory of old fights. 'Tis always so with you red men.[26] The old fields stir you, and here upon this ridge we fought your fight of rescue. God! what a rush we made! The air was full of hatchets as of acorns under shaken oaks when I burst through. I kicked an old skull under moss as we halted here, that she might not see it. It lies under that yellow tuft. I have ears, and I tell you nothing stirs. It is your superstition, chief. Neither living nor dead have passed to-night. A man without cross knows better. I will wait here till dawn. She said 'I would see sunrise in my face when I start for Mamelons,' and she shall. I have said."

To this the chief, after pause, signed back:

"I have stood the test, and from the burn-

---

[26] It is said that Indians cannot sleep upon a battlefield, however old, because of superstitious fear. They admit themselves that it is not well to do it, and always, under one excuse or another, avoid doing so.

ing stake went beyond flesh. I have seen the dead, and know them. I say the dead have passed to-night. Even as she danced her happy dances, and you laughed, I saw them crowd the ridge and come, filing downward. They fled with slanted spears. You know the sign. It was a warning, and for us and her. For, with the rest, heading the line, there walked two chiefs whose bosoms bore the Tortoise sign. I knew them. They slanted spears at her, and waved us down; then glided on at speed. And others yet I saw, not of my race —a woman floating in the air, her mother, clothed as she shall be to-morrow, and with her a long line of faces, like to hers asleep, save eager looking, anxious; and they, too, waved us downward toward the river. This is no riddle, trapper. It is plain. When do the dead move without cause? Awake your bride from dreams and come down. Some fate is flying with flat wings this way, I know not what. I only know the dead have waved me toward water, and I go."

So saying, he took the dark trail downward, and in the darkness disappeared.

"The spell is on him," muttered the trapper, as he sodded the brands, "and naught may stop him. The old fool will do some stumbling on the trail before his moccasins touch sand." And saying this, he gently kissed the sleeping girl, and taking her small hand in his strong palm, he fell asleep; sleeping upon the crumbling edge of fate and death, not knowing. Had he but known! Then might wedding bells, not wail, have sounded over Mamelons.

＊　　＊　　＊　　＊　　＊　　＊　　＊　　＊

"*Awake! awake! my God, the fire is on us, Atla!*" so roared he, standing straight.

Up sprang she, quick as a flash, and stood in the red light by his side, cool, collected, while with swift, steady hands, she clothed herself for flight. Then swept with haughty glance the flaming ridge and said: "The light that lights my way to Mamelons, my love, is hotter than sunrise; but we may head it." Then, with him, turned, and fled with rapid, but sure, feet down the smoking trail.

The fire was that old one which burnt itself into the memories of men so it became a birth-

mark, and thus was handed down to generations.[27] None knew how kindled. It first
flared westward of the shallow lake, where
Mistassinni empties its brown waters from the
north, and at the first flash flamed to the sky.
It is a mystery to this day, for never did fire
kindled in woods or grass run as it ran. It
raced a race of death with every living thing
ahead of it, and won against the swiftest foot
of man or moose. The whirring partridge,
buzzing on for life, tumbled, featherless, a
lump of singed, palpitating flesh, into the ashes.
The eagle, circling a mile from earth, caught
in the rising vortex of hot air, shrunk like a
feather touched by heat, and, lessening as he
dropped, reached earth a cinder. The living
were cremated as they crouched in terror or
fled screaming. The woods were hot as hell.
Trees, wet mosses, sodden mold, brooks,
springs, and even rivers, disappeared. Rocks

[27] It has been told me that many children born after the
terrible conflagration that had swept the forest from west of
Lake St. John to Chicoutimi, and which ran a course of
150 miles in less than seven hours, were marked, at birth,
as with fire.

cracked like cannon overcharged. The face of cliffs slid downward or fell off with crashes like split thunder. It was a fire as hot, as fierce, as those persistent flames which melt the solid core of the world.

Downward they raced in equal flight. Her foot was as the fawn's; his stride like that of moose. She bounded on. He swept along, o'er all. They spake no word save once. She slipped. He plucked her from the ground, and said: " Brave one, we'll win this race—speed on." She flashed a bright look back to him and flew faster. Thus, over boulders and round rocks, they sprang and ran. Above, the flying sheets of flame; behind, the red consuming line; around them, the horrid crackling of shriveling leaves; ahead, the water, nigh to which they were; when, suddenly, they ran into blinding smoke and lost the trail, and, tearing onward, without sight, she fell and, striking a sharp rock, lay still, numbed to weakness. The trapper, stumbling after, fell downward to her side, but his strong frame stood the hard shock, and staggered upward.

He felt for her, and found her limp. She knew his touch and murmured faintly, with clear tones: " Dear love, stay not for me : go on and live. Atla knows how to die."

He snatched her to his breast, and through his teeth, " *O God! have you no mercy?*" then plunged onward, running slanting upward, for the smoke was thick below, and he knew the trees grew stunted on the cliffs. He ran like madman. A saint running out of hell might not run swifter. He was in hell, the hell of fire ; with heaven, the heaven of cool, reviving water, just ahead. The strength of ten was in him, and it sent his body, with her body on his breast, onward like a ball. His hair crimped to the black roots of it. He felt it not. His skin blistered on cheek and hands. He only strained her closer to his bosom and tore on. With garments blazing, he whirled onward up the slope, streamed like a burning arrow along the ridge which edges the monstrous rock men call Cape Trinity, slid, tumbled, fell, down its smoking slope, until he came to where the awful front drops sheer ; then, heaving up his huge frame, still clasping her sweet weight within strong arms, plunged, like a burnt log rolling out of fire, into the dark, deep, blessed tide.

*　　*　　*　　*　　*　　*　　.*　　*

Morn came, but brought no sunrise. Smoke, black and dense, filled the great gorge, and hung pulseless over the charred mountains. Soot scummed the water levels, and new brooks, flowing in new channels, tasted like lye. Smells of a burnt world filled the air. The nose shrank from breath, and breathed expectant of offense. The fire brought death to ten thousand living things, and filled all the waste with stench of shallow graves, burnt skins, and smoldering bones.

The dead had saved the living, for the old chief lived. From the red beach he saw the trapper's race for life along the smoking ridge, and paddled quick to where he made his awful, headlong plunge into Eternity.[28] From the

---

[28] The recess of water curving inward toward the mountains between Cape Trinity and Eternity is called Eternity bay.

deep depths he rose, like a dead fish to surface,
his breath beaten out of him, but clasping still
in tight arms the muffled form. His tongueless
savior—so paying life with life, the old debt
wiped out at last—towed him to shore and on
the beach revived him with rude skill persistent. He came to sense with violence, torn
convulsively. His soul woke facing backward, living past life again. To feet he
sprang at his first breath, and yelled:
"*Awake! awake! my God, the fire is on us,
Atla!*" then plucked her from the sand where
she lay, weak, as a wilted flower, and started
with a bound to fly. The touch of her bent
form, drooping in his arms, recalled his soul
to sense, and he knew all, and reeled with the
woe of it. Down at the water's edge he sank,
cast covering cloth from head and hands,
bathed her dark face, and murmured loving
words to her still soul.

Through realms and spaces of deep trance
her spirit, lingering in dim void 'twixt life and
death, heard love's call, and struggled back
toward the shore of life and sense. From pulse-

less breast her soul clomb up, pushed the
fringed lids apart, and gazed, through wide
eyes of sweet surprise, upon his worshiped
face; then sank, leaving a smile upon her lips,
within the safe inclosure of deep sleep. All
day she slept within his arms. All night she
slumbered on. Wisely he waited, saying:
" Sleep to the overtaxed means life. It is the
only medicine, and sure. In sleep the wearied
find new selves."

But when the second morning after starless
night came to the world, she felt the waking
gray of it upon her lids, and, stirring in his
arms, like wounded bird in nest, moved mouth
and opened eyes, and gazed slowly round, as
seeking knowledge of place and time and circumstance. Then memory came, and she re-
membered all, and softly said, " Art thou
alive, dear love ? I have been with the dead.
The dead were very kind, but oh, I missed you
so," and with soft hand she stroked his face
caressingly. The old chief mutely stood,
watching, with gloomy eyes, the sad sight.
He read the motion of her lips, and in his

tongueless throat there grew a moan, and his
dry lids wet themselves with tears. She noticed
him and said: "You, too, alive, old servitor!
The gods are strict, but merciful. Two of the
three remain. The one alone must go. So is
it well." Then to her worshiped one: "Dear
love, this is a gloomy place. Let us go on.
The smoke hides the bright world. I long for
light. The fate is not yet sure. The blood of
our old race holds tightly to last chance. We
face it out with death to the last throb. Then
yield, not sooner. Who knows? I may find
sunrise yet at Mamelons."

So was it done.

They placed her on soft skins within the
boat facing him who steered, for she said:
"Dear love, the dead see not the living. If I
go I may not see you evermore. So let me
look on your dear face while yet I may. To-
day is mine. To-morrow—I know not who
may own to-morrow."

Thus, he at stern and she at stem, softly
placed on the piled skins, her dark eyes on
his face, they glided out of the deep bay.

round the gray base of the dread cape that stands eternal, and floated downward with the black ebb toward the sea. Past islands and through channels intricate, they went in silence, until they came to where the Marguerite, with tuneful mouth, runs singing over shining sands, pouring out into dark Saguenay, as life pours into death; then breathed they freer airs, and the freshness of untainted winds fell sweetly down upon them from overhanging hills, and thus she spake:

" Dear love, I know not what may be. We mortals are not sure of anything. The end of sense is that of knowledge. We know we live forever. For so our pride compels, and some have seen the dead moving. But under what conditions we do live beyond, we know not. Hence hate I death. It is an interruption and a stoppage of plans and joys which work and flow in sequence; severs us from loved connections; for the certain gives us the uncertain, and in place of solid substantial facts forces us to build our future lives on the unfixed and changeful foundations of hopes and dreams. It is not moral state that puzzles. We of the old race never worried over that. For we knew if we were good enough to live here, and once, then were we good enough to live elsewhere and forever; but it was the nature of existence, its environment, and the connections growing out of these, that filled the race whose child I am with dread and dole. For all the women of my race loved with great loves—the loves of lovers who sublimated life in loving, and knew no higher and no holier, nor cared to know. We cast all on that one chance; winning all in winning, and losing all if we lost. With me it is the same. I love you with a love that maketh life. I am a slave to it. It is my strength or weakness, as has been with the women of my blood from the beginning. I have no other creed, nor faith nor hope. To-day I see thee, and I have. To-morrow whom shall I see? The dead? I care not for the dead. There is not one among them I may love, for loving thee has cut me off from loving other one forever; unless the alchemy of death works back the creative process, undoing all of blood and nature, and sends us into nothingness, then brings us forth by new processes foreign to what we were, and wholly different from our old selves, which is a consummation horrible to think of."

"Nay, nay," exclaimed the trapper. "Such cannot be. Our loves, if they be large and whole, grow with us, and with our lives live on forever."

"It may be so, dear love," replied the girl. "Love's prophecy should be true as sweet, or else your sacred books are vain. For in them it is written, 'Love is of God.' But oh, how shall I find thee in that other world? · For wide and dim must stretch its spaces, and vast must be its intervals. This earth is small. We who live in it few. Within the circle of three generations all living stand. But the dead are many. The sands of Mamelons are not so numberless. They totalize the ages; the land, they dwell in beyond mortal compass. Who may be sure of meeting any one in such a realm? At what point on its boundaries shall I wait and watch? How signal thee, by hand or voice, when out of earth, like feather, blown, by that strange movement men call death, into the endless distances, thou comest suddenly.

"Alas! alas! I know not if beyond this day, I, going out of this dear sunlight, may ever and forever look upon thy face again!"

"Atla," returned the trapper, "I know not what may be. But this I know and swear, that if a trail pushed, seeking, through a thousand or ten thousand years, may bring me to thy side, we two shall meet in heaven."

"Oh, love, say those sweet words again," she cried. "Say more than them. Crowd into this one day, that I am sure of, the vows and loves of half a life, that I may go, if go I must, out of thy sight from Mamelons, heartful, upheld by an immortal hope. And here I pledge thee, by the Sacred Fire that burns forever, that if power bestowed by nature, or artfully acquired by patience working through ten thousand years, may find thee after death, then sometime will I find my heaven in thy

9

arms, not found till then. So, now, in holy
covenant we will rest until we come to Mamelons, and ever after.   I feel the breeze of wider
water on my cheek, and breathe the salted air.
I shall know soon if ever sunrise shine for me
at Mamelons."

So went they down in silence with the tide
that whirled itself in eddies toward the sea;
past L'Anse a l'Eau, where now the salmon
swim and spawn against their will,[29] past the
sharp point of rounded rocks, where sportively
the white whales[30] roll, and, steering straight
across the harbor's mouth, where her Basque
fathers anchored ships before the years of
men,[31] ran boat ashore where the great ledge

[29] At L'Anse a l'Eau, where the Saguenay steamers land
passengers for Tadousac, the tourist will find a fine collec-
tion of large salmon at the upper end of the little bay or recess, for here is one of the salmon hatching stations under
government patronage.

[30] The white whales, commonly called porpoises, are very
plentiful at the mouth of the Saguenay, and to a stranger
present a very novel and entertaining spectacle tumbling
in the black water. They are hunted by the natives for
both their skins and oil.

[31] Personally, I hold to the opinion that the eastern hemisphere never lost its knowledge of the western, but that,
from immemorial times, the Basques and their Iberian an-

runs, sloping down from upper sand to water, and shining beach and gray rock meet.

But as they crossed the harbor's mouth, sailing straight on abreast of Mamelons, its bright sands blackened and a shadow darkened on its front, and, as they bore her tenderly to the terrace, where stood tent and priest, a tremor shook the quivering earth, and through the darkening air a wave of thunder rolled.

"Dear love," she said, "it may not be. The fate still holds. The doom works out its dole. I may not be thy wife this side grave. What rights I have beyond I shall know soon. For soon the sight[32] will come to me, and what is hidden now will stand out plain." Then, lying on the skins, she gazed at Mamelons, looming

cestors visited at regular intervals the St. Lawrence, both gulf and river. Of course, the grounds on which I base such an opinion cannot be presented in this note.

[32] It is held by some that certain families have the power of "second sight," or to look into the future, come to them just before death. I have known cases where such power, apparently, did come to the dying. The Basque people held strongly to the belief that all of their kingly line were seers or prophets, and that, especially before dying, each had a full, clear view of the future.

vast and black in shadow, and, closing eyes, she prayed unto the gods, the earthborn, old-time fathers of her race.

But he could not have it so, and when prayer was ended said: "Atla, we have come far for marriage rite, and married we will be. Thou art mistaken. I have seen shadow settle and heard thunder roll before. In eye nor cheek are death's pale signals set. The holy man is here. Here ring and seal. Forget the doom, and let the words be read that bindeth to the grave."

To this she answering said: "Dear love, thou art in error, but thy word is law. My stay is brief. When yonder shadow passes I shall pass. There sleeps my father, and with him I must sleep. The earth is conscious. I am of those who were, earthborn, and so she feels our coming and our going as mother feels life and death of child. The sun is on the western hills. At sunset I shall die. But if it may stay up thy soul through the sad years, bid the good man go on."

Then took the priest his book, and, in the

language of the Latins, so old to us, so new beside her tongue, whose literature was dead a thousand years before Rome was, began to bind, by the manufactured custom of modern men, whose binding is of law and not of love, and hence a mockery. But ere he came to that sweet fragment of love's law and faith, stolen from the past, the giving and receiving of a ring, symbol of eternity, she suddenly lifted hand, and said :

" Have done! Have done! No need of marriage now. No need of rite, nor prayer, nor endless ring, nor seal of sacred sign. I see what is to be. The veil is lifted and I see beyond. I see the millions of my race lift over Mamelons. They come as come the seas toward shore, rolling in countless billows from central ocean. The old Iberian race, millions on millions, landscapes of moving forms, aligned with the horizon, come, marching on. Among them, lifted high, the gods. On thrones a thousand queens sit regnant, raimented like me. Their voice is as the sound of many waters.

" Last, best, and highest over all, we place
thee.

" The gods say so ? So be it, then. Mother,
I have kept charge. My love has won him.
The old race stops, but by no fault of mine. My
people, this man is lord and king to me. See
that ye bring him to my throne when he
comes seeking to the West. Dear love, you
will excuse me now. I must pass on; but
passing on I leave my soul with thee. Make
grave for me on Mamelons. Put lily at my
throat, green boughs on breast, bright sand
on boughs. Watch with me there one night.
I will be there with thee. So keep with Atla
holy tryst one night and only one—then go
thy way. We two will have sweet meeting
after many days." And saying this she put
soft hand in his and died.

Her lover, kneeling by her couch, put face
to her cold cheek, nor stirred. The holy man
said softly holy prayer; while the old tongueless chief of Mistassinni wrapped head in
blanket, and through the long night sat as one
dead.

Next day the silent man made silent grave on Mamelons. At sunset they brought her to it, raimented like a queen, and laid her body in bright sand; put lily at her throat, green boughs on peaceful breast, and slowly sifted clean sand over all.

That night a lonely man sat by a lonely grave, through the long watches keeping holy tryst. But when the sun came up, rising out of mists which whitened over Anticosti, he rose, and, standing, with bared head, he said:

"Atla,[33] we two will have sweet meeting

---

[33] I named my heroine Atla, because I hold that the Basques not only are descendants of the old Iberians, but that the Iberians were a colony from Atlantis. I accept fully Ignatius Donelly's conclusions as to the actual old-time existence of a great island continent in the Atlantic Ocean, and believe that in it the human race began and developed a civilization inconceivably perfect and splendid, of which the Egyptian, Peruvian, Iberian, and Mexican were only colonial repetitions. Atla is, therefore, the proper name for the last of the old Basque-Iberian blood to have, as it is the root of Atlantis (Atla-ntis), the original mother-land of all. I have never met Mr. Donelly, and may never meet him, and hence I make this opportunity to express the obligation I am under to him for entertainment and profit. The patience of the scholarship that could accumulate the material for a book like his "Atlantis" is worthy of a wider and more grateful acknowldgement than this

after many days." Then he went his way.

And there, on that high crest, whose sands first saw the sunrise of the world, when sang the stars of morning, beyond doom and fate, at last, the child of the old race, which lived in the beginning, sweetly sleeps at Mamelons.

superficial age of ours is able to give, for it cannot appreciate it. No man with any pretensions of scholarly attainments can afford to let "Atlantis" go unread.

www.ingramcontent.com/pod-product-compliance
Lightning Source LLC
Chambersburg PA
CBHW020746020726
47495CB00008B/2339